In It Together

Blood. Love. Sisters.

In It Together

EMILY BOURNE

First Published by Halo & Claws Publishing 2021

IN IT TOGETHER

For information contact: https://www.emilybourne.net

Stock Images via Bigstock, Shutterstock

ISBN: 978-1-925990-12-6 (Paperback)
ISBN: 978-1-925990-07-2 (Ebook)

1

Brittany

A dim yellow sun creeps around the border of my window blind.

His arm around me is for comfort, but all I feel is empty. I'd rather lay flat on my back, than squeezed against the edge of my single bed. The beds in our dorm rooms aren't big enough for two people. The rooms are hardly big enough for one person to live in.

His arm tightens around my mid-section and he stretches behind me. He's awake.

Bryce kisses behind my ear, and whispers, "Morning, beautiful."

I pat his arm and force my lips to curl. "Good morning."

He pulls himself up to sitting with a yawn. "Did you sleep ok?"

"Yes," I lie.

He leans over and kisses my lips. "That's good."

Bryce scoots out from under the covers and leapfrogs over me. He pulls on his pants and I hug the bed sheet around me.

"I've gotta get to class," he says. "I have training this afternoon, but d'you wanna meet up after?"

"Sure," I nod.

"Are you going to that dance class today?"

I swallow uncomfortably.

"Brit?"

"Yeah, I'll give it a go."

He swoops in to kiss my lips. "That's so good. You should get back into it. You loved dancing."

I bite my lip and nod. "I did."

"Ok, I really gotta go," Bryce says, pulling on his t-shirt. He grabs his keys and slides his phone into his back pocket. "I'll see you later."

I nod and smile. "See you."

Bryce leaves, and I flop on my back. I spread my arms and legs like a limp starfish. A weak sigh slithering out of me. I stare at the *badly-needing-a-paint-job* ceiling and try clearing my mind. Some pretty awful thoughts have spiralled inside there lately.

I check the time on my phone. I have an hour until my first class. It's contract law, so I'm not leaping out of bed to get there. I play with my shoulder-length, naturally sandy coloured hair, and contemplate the little interest I have in starting my day.

My phone buzzes in my hand.

Incoming Call - Mum.

Deep breath, and I hit answer. "Hey Mum."

"Morning Sweetheart. How is everything?"

"Yeah, good. Just getting ready for class."

"You sound sleepy."

"Just woke up."

"How are classes going?"

"Yeah, great."

Mum laughs. "Love the enthusiasm."

"You know I'm not a morning person. Why are you calling, anyway?"

Mum keeps laughing. "I can't call my daughter and check in?"

"You have another one you could call."

The laughter stops. "Brittany."

"What?"

"I want you to know how proud I am of you." There's a sharpness to her voice. "You are doing extremely well, and I see you going great places. Keep up the good work."

I twist my lips and nod. "Ok, Mum. Thanks."

"I'll let you get ready for class."

"Ok. Thanks for calling."

"I'll call again at the end of the week."

"Ok, bye."

"Love you, Sweetheart."

"Love you too."

We hang up and I stare at my phone. It's like she calls to remind me to not be like Charli.

Classes were as lacklustre as they normally are. I do well in classes. I retain the information fine. But I don't care about what I'm learning. There's no passion burning inside me.

That's why Bryce is pushing me to take a dance class. He sees it on my face. I'm almost expressionless these days. I have no oomph. No fire. I remember the days of dance classes. Especially when I changed to Tiffany's classes. After I warmed up, I ruled the dance group.

Then it was all snatched away.

After my last class, I dawdle through campus. There is a quiet tranquillity in the courtyards. The leafy foliage plays against the soft sun, and I almost forget how lonely I am in this place. I do love gazing at the academic architecture that holds a striking old world charm. It's what I imagine Cambridge or Paris might look like. It'd be nice to travel to the other side of the world one day. Immerse myself in the fashion of the people and the buildings.

"Hey Brittany," someone calls out to me.

I look away from the Arts & Science faculty, and Reece walks towards me, waving.

My veins energize in a way I haven't felt in months.

I smile as I reply, "Reece, hi. How are you?"

He nods. "Good. I'm heading to another class, but good to see you."

"You too," I say as he passes me.

A slow exhale dwindles out of me. I wish I saw him more often. I wish I saw anyone more often.

Do I have any friends besides Bryce?

The dance class I'm attending is beginner's jazz. I remember taking jazz with Charli when I was eight-years-old. It was fun, but Charli got bored. She hated being told how to move. Mum and Dad got sick of us bickering, and took us both out of the class. I stuck to ballet and Charli did her tomboy activities I wasn't interested in.

"Welcome Brittany," a woman of about forty with chunks of hot pink in her hair, says after I introduce myself. "Glad to have you with us. Have you done any dance classes before?"

"No." I'm hopeful I've remembered moves from my prior lessons and can wow them. But basically, I'm terrified my moves will be horrible.

"That's ok, we're all beginners here. My name is Melody."

I smile a reply and move towards the rest of the beginners group.

Having Melody as our instructor makes me feel a little more comfortable. If a forty-year-old is showing us the moves, surely I can keep up. Sometimes my hip or part of my leg will have a flare up. I'm hoping I don't aggravate it.

Melody walks us through four steps. I trip on my feet. With annoyance, I shake my head. I recall doing this pre-accident. It was easy. It's ok, Brittany, we can get through this.

The girl beside me picks it up easily. I notice my scowl and quickly drop it. She's done this before. She's not a beginner.

I'm not a beginner.

But I'm not getting this.

Melody shows us another four steps. It hurts when I twist. Should I tell Melody about the surgeries? I scan the group. I don't want pity in their eyes.

Pity is the worst.

Sanford is full of pity. I hate going back home. I see it in Mum's eyes. My dad's eyes. Tara's eyes. My step-siblings' eyes.

But not Charli. Charli is busy fighting the eyes of disapproval and disappointment. When she looks at me, determination fills her gaze.

I miss her.

Ouch!

A stinging pain burns my hip. I slump to my right, trying to stand straight. But it hurts.

"You right?" the girl beside me asks.

I fake a smile and nod. With a clenched jaw, I try the sequence in time with Melody. I'm three beats behind.

A red heat of frustration and embarrassment inflames my skin. As Melody turns to the sound system to restart the track, I back away. I pick up my bag and move towards the door.

"You're not leaving?" Melody calls out.

I look over my shoulder and I'm sweating.

"It doesn't have to be perfect," she says. "It's the first day."

I purse my lips and turn the door handle. My heart thuds as I leave the dance studio.

It was a massive mistake being there. I knew it before going. Maybe I did it more for Bryce than myself. Since being at uni, he's been doing so well health-wise and socially. He hates the pity from Sanford, too. There, he's the boy whose mum died. He's the boy with the eating disorder. The boy on antidepressants.

Here, he has a fresh start. I'm running out of fingers to name all the new friends he's made. I want to keep up with him and be by his side. But, in this place, I don't feel like me. Classes are mundane. I don't know why I still go to them. To get a piece of paper? So Mum and Dad will like me?

I sit on a bench in the courtyard by the arts centre and scroll through my phone. It's only a few minutes until Bryce will meet me. I need time to cool down. Otherwise, he'll see straight through me, and know the dance class was a disaster.

"Hey Britty," he says, sliding beside me and kissing my forehead. "How was the dance class?"

I bite my lip and nod. "It was fun."

"You'd go back?"

"Maybe."

"What's wrong?"

"Nothing."

"What's with the, *maybe*?"

I shrug. "It was just a different style to what I used to do."

"Do you wanna find a different class?"

I nod. "Maybe."

He squeezes my hand. "Britty, you look sad."

I look away from him. "I had a flare up."

He exhales, drooping forward. "I'm sorry. Could you get through the class?"

A prick of tears threatens to break. "Kinda."

"Maybe it's just your body easing into it. After some practice, you'll feel like your old self."

Old self? Are you serious? "You might be right."

"Do you want to go to a party with me? Johnny's putting it on. You like him, right?"

My chest constricts. "You want me to go?"

His finger curls under my chin. "Of course I want you to go."

I jerk my head back. "I dunno."

"Why?"

"I limped back from the dance class."

"Oh." He drops his hand.

"You go, though. You'll have fun."

I can tell he wants to smile, but doesn't for my benefit. He's really put himself out there at uni, and I'm happy for him. Sometimes, I feel like I hold him back. Part of me wants to hold him back.

"I can stay with you," he offers.

I smile and shake my head. "No. Seriously. You go and have fun."

Here, he's the boy who has fun. He's the boy with the *stick-in-the-mud* girlfriend. He's the boy who's too good to be with her.

Tonight, I sit alone in my dorm room. Bryce is at the party. I mean it when I say I'm happy for him. I just don't know what I'm doing.

What is the meaning of my life? I don't know why I don't

talk to him about this. My gut clamps at the thought of talking to anyone about this.

I want this feeling to go away. I'm sick of feeling so blah.

So nothing.

So meaningless.

2

Charli

I thwack the nail with my hammer. The energy of my swing ricochets up my arm and quakes in my shoulder. I rub my shoulder and my other hand grips the hammer. Perhaps that was too much force. But dammit, I wanna be done for the day.

"Got some anger to take out, Charli?" Peter sniggers beside me.

I pick up another nail and smirk. "No, just a long day."

Peter gathers supplies left strewn across the ground by other volunteers. "We'll call it a day soon."

I line up the nail and shrug. "It's not a problem, just my stomach protesting for food."

Peter laughs as he walks past me. "Tina is making tacos

tonight."

"Don't tell me that," I whine, grinning. "Now my stomach will really start punching me."

Peter is our volunteer coordinator and rarely jokes. Must be the fact the project is winding up, he's finally loosening up.

This is my second project with *Habitat For Humanity*. The monsoon in this part of Thailand was catastrophic. It breaks my heart, these horrific natural disasters happen in parts of the world already struggling. This village doesn't have the means or money to clean up and rebuild. Thank goodness for organisations like this.

I don't understand why more people don't help. Like the people in Sanford who have too much money. They could donate. Hell, it'd be a tax write-off. But, no. Every time I raise money for one of these trips, people back home totally ignore the plea.

Don't even get me started on my parents.

No university. No attention. No admiration.

What a load of shit. I take action now. But, apparently, a piece of paper after four years of study is the only thing that matters.

I whack another nail. I shouldn't think about home. It always works me up, and I don't think my shoulder can handle the brunt of more hits.

I drop the hammer on top of the box of nails and wipe my hands together. They're sore with a red shine. Mostly my hands are dirty. *Ick.* I wipe them along my jeans, which are already filthy, and move towards the water bucket.

I scrub my hands in the communal bucket and look over to Sally, who's fumbling with her hammer and missing the nail. On purpose?

"Sal? You ok?" I call out.

Sally looks over her shoulder at me and blushes.

I can't help laughing. "Whaddaya doing?"

She smirks. "I hit my thumb earlier and now I'm shit-scared to hit the nail."

"Ouch. Sorry about that." I make my way over to her. "Want me to do it?"

"I gotta nail in these three spots. But I don't wanna be a bother."

I snort a laugh and hold my hand out. "Gimme it."

Sally laughs and hands over the hammer. "You're a lifesaver, mate."

I met Sally on the plane ride over to Thailand. We're the only Australians in the group. She's such a crack up. Sometimes when I'm missing home, I hang with Sally and she'll say something so *bogan* it makes me stop missing home. Just looking at her makes me laugh. She has the funniest facial expressions.

"Think the families will like their new digs?" Sally asks, hands in pockets as she gazes around the nearly finished home.

"I'm sure they will."

"Sad but isn't it."

"How so?"

"This is the best we can do for them."

"Shelter is shelter," I say, hitting the last nail. "When you have nothing, you're grateful for the smallest things."

Sally shrugs and takes the hammer back. "Too right, mate."

I smile and make my way towards Tina and the food. "Heard we got tacos tonight," I call out.

Tina smiles over her outdoor stove. "I knew they would bring you over."

I stop beside her and take a big whiff. I nudge her and grin. "Can't get enough of me, huh?"

Tina purses her lips, trying to hide her giddy smile. "Make yourself useful," she says, handing me a wooden spoon. "Stir the mince while I bring out the salad."

"Ok boss," I say, stepping in front of the stove.

As I stir, Peter stops by and sniffs. "Not bad," he says with approval.

"Not my doing," I say. "Mine would never smell this good."

Peter steals the wooden spoon from me and attempts to eat a spoonful.

I hit his hand. "Whaddaya crazy. Tina would kill us both if she caught you doing that."

Peter laughs and hands me back the spoon.

Tina returns and lets me plate up first. I then snag a place on a log closest to the fire that Ryan is attempting to keep a light.

"Want some help?" I ask him.

"Nah, I got it," he says with a wink.

"Good," I reply, "cause I wanna eat."

I hold my taco, careful to not let anything ooze out and drip down my hand. I'd like to not be a total grub this dinner.

"Hey cutie," Kumi chirps as she bounces down beside me.

I'm occupied with a mouthful of taco, so don't respond.

Kumi kisses behind my ear, the sweet and breathy way she does. Fuck. I love when she does that.

Taco sauce drizzles down my hand. Shit. Kumi is *uber* distracting.

"Yummy?" Kumi whispers in my ear.

I giggle as I try to swallow. I swallow everything despite the gorgeous distraction whose hands play at my torso. "Yes, it is. I don't want to put it down or it'll get too messy."

"I like messy," Kumi says and leans into my taco and takes a bite.

Hot.

"Excuse me," I say. "Get your own."

Kumi covers her mouth as she chews and suppresses her giggles.

I love how round her cheeks are. The reflection of the fire flickers in her dark, round eyes. Everything about her face is round. Kissing her is like making out with a cutesy manga character.

I nudge her. "Seriously, go before Tina runs out. And snag me another one."

"Ok." Kumi gets up and skips towards Tina and the food.

Kumi went to an American high school, so her English is fantastic. But best believe I started my bond with this gorgeous Japanese girl by gushing about all the anime I love. She's told me about all the places in Japan I should visit, and all the great dishes I should try. I am booking a trip over there ASAP. Visiting Kumi will be a monumental perk.

I'll miss her when our project is over.

Kumi races back beside me. "Tina didn't let me take extra."

"*Pa-ha*! What?"

Kumi shrugs. "She said no."

"Did you say it was for me?"

Kumi nods with a mouthful.

I squint my eyes and lean around the fire to glimpse Tina.

Tina holds her hips and eyes me. "Don't make your girlfriend do your dirty work," she calls out.

I laugh and place my plate beside me. I kick my legs out and stretch my arms over my head. "Maybe I've had enough, anyway."

Kumi laughs and nudges me. "You're just being lazy."

I laugh. "Shuddup."

"Wanna stay in my tent tonight?" Kumi asks.

I nod. "Yep, sure."

Kumi nestles closer to me. "Yay."

Geez, she's cute.

I take mine and Kumi's plates to wash up. I nod at Tina. "See, I do her dirty work, too."

Tina smirks as she scrubs a pan.

After I wash and dry the plates, I hear my name called. My eyes land on Jensen and suddenly I feel flushed.

He beckons me over. "Hey," he says.

"Hey," I say, walking over to him.

"We're leaving soon," he says in his deep Texan accent.

I bite inside my cheek and nod. "Sure are."

His hands run along my shoulders and down my arms. "I'll miss you, girl." He always calls me girl.

"I'll miss you too. One day I'll make it to the States. It's on the list."

His eyebrow lifts. "Higher on the list than Japan?"

I sigh. "Don't start with me."

His arms encircle me and one of his hands cheekily cups my bum.

"Don't," I whisper, batting his hand away.

"I thought you weren't into serious dating?"

"I'm not."

"So, what does it matter if you spend tonight with me instead of her?"

I shrug. "She already asked me."

"And, I'm asking you now."

"Stop it. She's not into sleeping with more than one person on a trip."

"But you are."

"Look, it was fun with you, but I'd rather be with Kumi." I push away from him. "Like you said, I do what I want."

Jensen scoffs. "Put it like it is then."

"Well, you're not exactly sweeping me off my feet right now." Typical man. Grab a girl's arse, it'll magically make her want you.

"All right. But before we leave Thailand, we need to catch up." He winks. "For old time's sake."

"I'll think about it."

I clasp my hands together as I walk back to the fire. Back to Kumi. When I first got to camp, I hooked up with Jensen. He's a player. He's great in bed, but out of bed, it's painful to hear him speak.

I sit down next to Kumi and she steals my arm, tracing the quill tattooed on my forearm. "I love looking at your body," she says. "It's like an art gallery I'm allowed to touch." She leans in and does that breathy kiss behind my ear. "And lick," she whispers.

A wave of goosebumps shiver me from head to toe. Can we go to her tent now?

She pats my thigh. "I wanna see the phoenix again. The blues and oranges are so gorgeous."

"Just wait," I whisper. "I'm not taking my pants off in front of everyone."

Kumi cups her mouth, giggling.

I love her giggle.

She squeezes my hand. "Let's go."

I nod and stand with her.

Ok, so this is a weird thing to say about someone you're having sex with, but Kumi reminds me so much of Brittany. I'm weirding myself out so much right now. But she reminds me of the old Brittany. Giggly. Bashful. Passionate. Hopeful. Funny. I like being around Kumi for the memories of pre-accident Brittany.

I take Kumi's hand away from tracing the roses tattooed on my ribs, and kiss it. "Would you be able to translate something into kanji for me? It's for a new tattoo."

Her eyes widen and sparkle. "Of course. Where will this one be?"

I tap the space above the inside of my elbow. "A place nice

and visible."

"Will you get it in Thailand? So I can go with you?"

"Sure. Will you get your first tattoo?"

Her cheeks grow rosy. "Ah, I dunno." She squeezes my thigh. "I'm not daring enough to get badass tattoos like you."

She traces the phoenix rising from the flames, etched into the skin on my thigh.

"The hesitation quivering your voice sounds like a yes," I tease.

Kumi bites her lip and rolls on top of me. "Just shut up and kiss me."

I run my hands through her hair. *My pleasure.*

3

Brittany

The best year of my life was when I was sixteen-years-old. I scroll through my *Instagram* page and my stomach twists. Parties, drinking, dancing, cheerleading, and popularity filled grade ten. The grade eleven feed is almost non-existent, and then grade twelve morphs into this tame version of my life.

Grade twelve was hardly *my life*.

This is hardly my life.

I kneel on my dorm room floor, clutching my phone with trembling hands. The sweat builds and I drop the phone. Bile creeps up my throat and knots climb my spine. I pick up the blade and swallow hard.

Tears flood my eyes as I stare at the razor blade in my palm. There's no meaning to my life. I don't why I'm doing this anymore.

Just do it, Brittany.

Bryce is miserable with me. He's embarrassed by me.

Do it.

I sniff back the runny mucus in my nose and lean forward with a gut-tearing moan. This isn't my life. That car crash took it away from me. Now I have someone else's life. I have what Charli wanted.

Do it.

I never wanted this. It's not fair. I wanted my fun life, but I'm stuck with this to keep my parents happy. I can't live my life for them. What's the point? I can't live my life.

I can't live my life.

Just do it, Brittany!

Do it!

Do it!

I scream and run the blade across my wrist, slicing my vein.

An intense, searing pain runs from my wrist to my brain. Blood gushes from the cut.

Shit.

"No!" I scream at my wrist. I hold my hand over the cut and race to my wardrobe. I pull out the closest item and hold it over the blood draining from my wrist. The blood oozes into the fabric and my woozy head spins.

I move around my bed, almost slipping in blood, and race to the door. I run out of my room and down the hall, and bash myself against my R.A.'s door.

I bash and bash, screaming, "Nell! Nell!"

Nell reefs her door open. "What the hell?"

"Please help me!" I scream at her, lifting the reddened fabric around my forearm.

"Shit, what happened?"

"I had an accident."

My whole body convulses with adrenaline.

Nell's hands hover around mine. "Is it a deep cut?"

"I dunno," I panic. "It happened with a blade."

"I'm judging whether it's a trip to a campus nurse, or an emergency room visit."

"I just need help. I'm gonna pass out."

Nell gently clasps my shoulders. "It's ok. You're going to be ok."

My vision doubles.

"Brit?" Nell's voice distorts. "Brittany, are you ok?"

Nell's expression sets in realisation of what I did. My stomach flips, twists, and tears. My vision triples and then completely blurs. Everything goes white.

Fuck.

"Brittany," a voice whispers.

I flutter my eyes open and everything is white.

Fuck.

"Brittany."

Someone grabs my hand. I flinch and turn my head to the right. Nell smiles at me.

"Hi," I whisper, shrinking into the bed.

Bed. I'm in a bed. There's a beeping beside me. I hate that

beeping. I'm in hospital.

Fuck.

I said I'd never be back in a hospital.

"How are you feeling?" Nell asks.

I shrug a response.

"You weren't out for long," she says. "Do you want me to call someone for you?"

"No," I rush.

She backs off. "Ok."

I blink hard and pull myself up. Hang on... it's not a hospital. "Where am I?"

Ouch. My head. Uh, I'm so groggy. But just the thought of blood can spin me out.

Blood.

So much blood.

"It's the first aid station by the Administration," Nell says. "We came here so my friend Tia could sew you up."

Not computing. "Huh?"

"Your wrist," Nell points to me. "You were talking to Tia. You don't remember?"

"Who is Tia?"

"My friend who is a nursing student," Nell says slowly. "I texted her to meet us here. You really were woozy. You don't remember?"

I move my arm and look down at my wrist, which is wrapped in a bandage. I clench my jaw and stare hard at the fluorescent lights.

Fuck.

"I don't remember anything since the hall. How did I get here?"

"We walked together."

"I walked?"

"Yes."

"I thought I fainted by your door."

"You were a bit tripped out, but I kept ya upright." She pats my shoulder. "You'll be right, Brit. Probably the panic attack wiped your short term memory."

"What was that beeping I heard?"

"What beeping?" Nell asks, squinting as she looks around the room. She points out the door. "There's a photocopier just out there. Maybe that's what you heard."

I settle back down on the bed. "*Phew.* I was scared I was back in hospital."

"You don't like hospitals?"

"I hate them."

A woman walks into the room, a bright smile on her face and her jet black hair pulled back into a loose bun.

"Hello," she says with a wave. "I'm Nurse Tanner, one of Tia's tutors. Do you mind if I check on her work?"

"She won't get into trouble for doing this, will she?" Nell says in a panic. "I wanted Brittany helped as quickly as possible."

Nurse Tanner's cheery smile brightens, and she lifts a hand to halt Nell's edginess. "Of course not. Tia's more than capable of some stitch work. She told me the cut wasn't too deep. I just want to check on the patient." She nods at me. "You're Brittany?"

I nod hesitantly.

She sits beside me. "Can you tell me what happened?"

I exhale quickly and gaze at the ceiling.

What happened? I don't know what happened. I can't talk about not knowing what happened.

"You were very lucky," Nurse Tanner adds. "A little higher and you would have cut into a vein."

I missed the vein? Thank goodness.

"It was an accident," I whisper.

"How did it happen?" she asks gently.

"I was crafting," it just comes out. "I was cutting fabric and not paying attention. I think my phone rang or something. Anyway, I moved the blade and got my arm."

When I sewed in high school, I'd have this reoccurring thought, one day that would happen for real.

"So, it wasn't on purpose?"

My skin is so pale I feel frozen inside.

"Why would I do it on purpose?" my voice is so small.

She pats my arm. "Of course. Why would you."

I swallow and taste bile. It's unsettling the way she looks at me. Does Nell think I did it on purpose too?

I did do it on purpose.

Why did I do it on purpose?

"Take some time before getting up," Nurse Tanner says. "Don't rush yourself."

"I'll walk her back to her room," Nell says.

Shit... I did it on purpose?

4

Charli

The worst part about travelling overseas is walking through Sydney Airport arrivals lounge. Everyone else walks through and loved ones greet them. Couples embrace with kisses. Families call out names and pull embarrassing dance moves. Friends snap the perfect *Instagram* post.

And here I am. Every time. Alone.

I readjust my backpack and walk through the crowds. Once I'm home, I'm fine. It's just this smack of reality, showing what is lacking in my life.

Oh well, I can't change it. I can't change them. They cut me out. If they change their attitude, I'd gladly include them in my life. Right now, I have to accept the fact I'm estranged from my parents.

"Charli," a voice calls.

My heart leaps into my throat. Me?

I look around and almost fall backwards. It's Harrison. His gorgeous smile, wild hair, and stubbly face.

My smile electrifies as he walks towards me.

"Hi," I say, embracing him in a hug. I notice his backpack. "Did you just get back from somewhere?"

"No, I just flew in from Melbourne," he says, pulling out of the hug. "I'm transferring and hopping on a plane to Chile."

"Oh, wow. I haven't been, yet."

"You have to. The people, the culture, the food, the landscape. You'll love it."

"My travel list is already a mile long," I joke.

"You just got back from somewhere?"

"Thailand. Just finished a building project."

He caresses my cheek. "That's awesome. I knew you'd do great things."

I shrug, hoping not to blush. "It's baby-steps."

"It's help, and that's all that matters." He smiles, shaking his head. "Damn, why am I seeing you before jumping on a plane? Do you have frequent flyer points to spend? Jump on the plane to Chile with me?"

I bite into my lip as I grin. "No, sorry. Maybe we will be in the same country in a few months?"

"Maybe," he replies. "I'll email you."

He walks backwards, his arm lifted in a wave.

"Travel safe," I call as he disappears into the crowd.

I'm not holding my breath on an email. His quickest replies

take six months.

After dropping my gear off at my apartment and taking a much needed shower, I leave for the hair salon. I loved being in Thailand, but my hair did not. I have so much blonde regrowth. It was fine the past few weeks having no mirrors, but now I can't stand it. I need every strand to be one-hundred percent brunette. Plus, there's so much dirt and ick on my scalp, I just want to pay someone to get rid of it.

We didn't have the best bathrooms whilst on the project. Let's just say a hose doesn't have the best water pressure.

"*Habitat For Humanity*? Wow, that's crazy awesome," my hair stylist, Viv, says as she combs through my hair. "How was it?"

"It was really fulfilling. One of the best parts is the people you meet."

"You mean, like, locals?"

"Yeah, they're fantastic. But I also mean the other volunteers."

"Oh, yeah. Like-minded and what not?"

"Exactly."

"You have such beautiful curls," Viv says, playing with my hair that stretches below my elbows. "Are you sure you want to blow-dry it?"

"Please." I nod at the mirror. "Get rid of the curls."

I run my finger over the new ink inside my arm. I'm so glad Kumi translated it. It's guaranteed to not say something random, like onions. These three little symbols are beyond precious to me.

Now, I have a piece of Kumi with me. However, the overall meaning is much more special.

I laugh under my breath. I wish I could have convinced Kumi to get a tattoo. That would have been awesome. I'm so glad I didn't see Jensen after the project ended. There was something about him that seemed so controlling. I don't need that in my life. It was nice to spend the last few days with Kumi before heading home.

After the salon, I return home with a takeaway Pad Thai. I don't know why I got Thai food. The stuff here can't compare with real-deal Thai food.

"You're back," my roommate, Naomi, says with little interest, as she takes a bottle of juice from the fridge.

"Yeah, couple of hours ago."

"Jetlagged?" she asks, walking back to her bedroom.

I'd answer 'not yet,' but she has already shut her door. I sit on a kitchen stool, open my laptop, and twirl my chopsticks around the noodles.

I open mywords.com and log in. I have fourteen notifications. Fourteen users liked my last poem. My lips curl as I read over the comments.

This hit me with all the feels.

You're a beast with words. Fucking love your stuff.

You should be published. Seriously, who are you? I want to

Published? Anthologies? I prefer the anonymity of mywords.com, rather than people knowing this stuff is written by Charlotte Matthews. Let's stick with *@phoenixrising* for now.

I tap the edge of my keyboard, thinking about my run in with Harrison. I'll never forget him. The boy I lost my virginity to in the forest. My first time in the forest since Kellie's death. Harrison helped me become whole again.

I'll always be grateful for him.

But now my love life is like an open-door policy. If you can even call it love. Kumi didn't believe in sleeping around. She would only consent if I promised to only be with her. We weren't official or anything, but I did keep my promise. But my day-to-day life... There are kinda no rules. People come and go from my bed, and there are newcomers at the most unexpected times. I just don't know if a committed relationship is for me.

My forehead twinges. Damn. The jetlag is setting in. I close my laptop, hitch it under my arm and take my Pad Thai to my bedroom.

As I sit cross-legged on my bed, digging the chopsticks into the paper box, I smirk. Imagine if Sophia caught me eating in bed. She'd absolutely flip her lid.

When half the box is empty, I sit it on my bedside table. I recline against the pillows and unlock my phone. I scroll through *Instagram*, glimpsing images of people I've met from all over the globe. The friends and the lovers. Many of whom I explore myself with, and use to forget one person.

The more I'm with others, it makes it ok that I'm not with him. That I can't be with him. Helps to forget how much I miss him. How much I want him.

I'm not following his *Instagram*, but I carefully stalk his page now and then. He looks happy. There's the same shine to his lower lip as he smiles. The same dark wild in his eyes. His image sends me comfort, warmth, and apprehension, just as it did all those years ago.

He has rarely posted this year, but I don't mind looking at the same images over again. It's like freezing time. A time where it'd be ok if we were together.

I close my eyes, nestle on the covers of my bed, and slide my hands into my pants. I bite my lip, smiling, as Travis's face coats my mind.

5

Brittany

I turn and sigh at Charli's apartment building. My stomach flips. I swallow and push for a smile. Seeing her has to make everything ok.

I lean my weight on the walking cane and slowly take the steps leading up to the front door. At least there is an elevator inside.

I knock on her door. No answer. I knock again and lean close to the door, trying to hear movement inside. Should I knock again?

Mid-knock, the door opens. I stumble as the door reefs away from my ear.

"Yes?" Charli's roommate answers. "Oh, you're the twin. She's not here."

"You mean Charli?"

She leans against the door, blocking the entry. "Yeah, she's at work. Find her there."

I gulp uncomfortably. "Ok, thanks."

She rolls her eyes and pushes the door close. "Bye then."

I move back towards the elevator. Holding the cane really hurts with the bandage around my left wrist. Well, it hurts because of the bruising and cut underneath the bandage. My hip and my shin are throbbing today. I texted Bryce I was on my period, and spent a few days in bed, sleeping away my thoughts. Perhaps not comfortable, but what else was I gonna do?

Back on the street, I search for another bus. I need to go straight to Charli's work, otherwise I'll chicken out completely.

As I limp my way towards the bar of *Sully's* where Charli works, I'm nervous at the sight of her. Her dark brown hair is pinned back in a neat bun, she has natural-looking makeup, a long-sleeved white blouse that covers her tattoos, and a brown, hipster bow tie and apron. It is so not her. *Sully's* is an upmarket restaurant and bar, the kinda place Charli wouldn't go as a paying customer. But she likes it because she can leave without notice to go overseas, and when she comes back, they always have shifts for her.

She lifts her head and her eyes twinkle as a happy grin brightens her face. "Oh my goodness, Brittany! What are you doing here?"

"Hi," I whisper with shyness, edging towards the bar.

Her smile weakens a little when noticing my cane. "You're

using that again?"

I shrug it off, hiding it and my wrist out of view below the bar. "Just a little flare up. How are you? How was your trip?"

She nods, her smile lifting again. "So good. We had a really great group. It was sad to leave."

"Must have been hard work," I say, pushing myself onto a bar stool.

"It was, but helps when you can see the big picture. Those villagers will be thrilled with their new homes."

"I'll bet."

"So, why are you here?" she asks, polishing a wine glass. "Don't you have classes?"

I shrug. "I can miss a few."

Charli lowers the glass and stares hard into my eyes. "What's wrong?"

"Huh?"

"You seem really down. Like, more than really down."

I purse my lips and tilt my gaze to my lap, as a lump balls in my throat.

"Brittany?"

I blink at the water coating my eyes.

"Is it your hip? Your leg?" Charli tries. "Not Bryce? You guys didn't have a fight, did ya?"

I sigh out. I can't look at her.

She leans closer. "Brit?"

I let go of the cane and lift my left arm. I place it on the bar as Charli asks, "*Whoah*, what happened?"

I turn my arm so the inside of my wrist is visible.

Charli runs her hand over the bandage. She says nothing for a few moments. She begins a few sentences, but the nonsensical sounds don't lead anywhere.

When I get the courage to meet her eyes, she shakes her head and blurts, "You didn't do this to yourself, did you?"

My lip quivers and Charli pushes back from the bar, rushing to the side entry. "Dane, cover the bar for me," she calls out, and suddenly her arms are around me. "Come to a booth with me."

I nod and slide off the stool. I hold the cane but most of my weight is on Charli. She leads me to a booth. When we sit, she waits for me to talk.

"I can't," I whisper.

Her eyes widen. "You can't what?"

"Explain."

She breathes out slowly. "Ok. When did it happen?"

"Three days ago."

Charli rubs her wrist and frowns. "I should have called you. I had this stabbing pain in my wrist on the plane back, but thought I'd slept on it wrong. Ah, I should have known."

I intertwine my fingers on the tabletop, trying to not relive anything in my head.

"Where were you those three days?" Charli asks, the trepidation on her face showing fear I'll say, 'in hospital.'

"I was in bed. Ignored my phone and didn't go to classes. People will think I did it on purpose."

Her head tilts backward. "You didn't?"

My jaw clenches.

She shakes her head. "Sorry, I shouldn't have said that. Of

course you didn't."

I plant my hands on the table. "I haven't cut myself before."

Charli takes my hand. "Of course. Of course, you haven't."

"I'm not crazy or anything."

She squeezes my hand. "I know that. Why would you say that?"

"I got help right away by choice. I'm not crazy."

Charli clears her throat and fidgets, still holding my hand. "So, if you didn't do this..." She gestures at the bandage. "How did it happen?"

I look from her, to my wrist, to her. "I did the cut."

Her jaw tenses like she's biting inside her cheek. Her brow furrows and her eyes shine with uneasy tears.

"Don't look at me like that."

"Brit, I don't understand what's happening."

I pull my hand away. "Nothing's happening."

Charli leans in and whispers. "You never randomly visit me. Something major has happened. Did you come here to talk, or not?"

Tears stream from my eyes and loud sobs rush out before I can stop them. I cup my mouth as my shoulders shake. Hurt rises from my stomach and grasps my heart.

Charli's arms wrap me up and she brings my head to her shoulder. I gasp for air as the sobs choke my throat. She hushes me, telling me it's ok. I close my eyes tight, trying to stop the tears.

I finally breathe. I lift my head and wipe my eyes.

"You ok?" she whispers.

Another cry whimpers out of me. I keep my head down and say, "I can't keep pretending. I can't pretend to live this life."

Charli's hands shake as she holds me. Her voice wavers, "What?"

I slide my hands over my face.

"Shit." Charli lets me go and scoots out of the booth. "Where's Mike?" she calls out.

"Dunno," the guy behind the bar calls back.

"Tell him I have to go."

"What?"

"My sister needs me."

"You've got another four hours of your shift."

"Get him to call someone in to cover."

"Charli," I whisper. "It's ok. I can go home."

"Forget it," she whispers back. "I'm taking you home."

A smile tingles my lips and relief coats my body.

"Take a seat on the couch," Charli says as we enter her apartment. "I'll brew a pot of tea."

I amble my way to the couch as Charli opens cupboards in the adjacent kitchen.

"What's the racket?" a roommate says, walking out of her bedroom.

"Just making tea," Charli says, not looking at the girl. "You want a cup?" I can tell she doesn't mean it.

The girl grunts as she takes a bottle of the water from the fridge. She turns and trudges back to her bedroom.

"Is your roommate always this friendly?"

Charli shakes her head. "Don't even go there."

As Charli prepares the tea that I don't particularly want, I fidget in place. Everything is uncomfortable. My clothes, my mood, my life.

"You could have called for me right away," Charli says, pouring boiling water into the teapot.

"I didn't know you were back. It's not like we talk that much."

"I'm your twin."

"*Exactly*," I snap. "You're my twin and I never know what's going on with you."

Charli taps a foot against a kitchen cupboard. "You really feel like that?"

I shrug. "I just miss you."

Charli rushes toward me. "I miss you too." She sits beside me. "I miss you so much."

"Then why don't you talk to me?"

"What do you mean? I don't ignore you."

"I find out about your holidays by scrolling through *Instagram*."

Charli recoils slightly. "I figured you had sided with Mum and Dad."

"What?" I scoff.

"I thought you didn't want to know about my life because I didn't go to uni with you."

I frown. "I couldn't give a shit about uni."

"I've lived here for almost a year and you've visited max of three times," she whispers. "How was I supposed to know you missed me?"

"I was trying to adapt to life at university. I thought shutting you out would help…" Sigh. "It didn't."

"Help with what?"

I reach for her hand and she latches on. "Fitting in. Living somewhere new." Even bigger sigh. "Making Mum and Dad happy. Proud."

"Oh, fuck them." She slaps a hand over her mouth. "Sorry, that came out before I thought it."

I smirk. "You're right. Fuck em."

Charli puffs a laugh which is layered with surprise. "Since when do you swear?"

"I seem to do it a lot lately."

Charli slides onto the couch beside me. "Not to sound like an alarmist, but something seems very wrong."

I flop my head on her shoulder. "I hate my life."

"Brit." Her voice is a breathy heartache. "You'll stay with me. We'll work this out."

She plays with my hair, and I reply, "Ok." I don't have to ask her to not tell our parents. She's already not speaking with them. I wonder when Mum or Dad last called Charli. It's too awkward to ask them. If Charli were in my shoes, she would have already asked.

"I just feel stuck," I tell her.

"At school?"

"Yeah. And empty. There's no meaning to anything I'm doing."

"You don't like studying law?"

"It's fine. But I want more than fine."

Charli hugs me tighter. "So you should."

"It's more than school, it's my whole life that leaves me feeling blank. You're so lucky."

"Lucky?"

"You're doing what you want. You're brave. Way braver than me."

"I am not lucky. I'm alone. My family abandoned me."

I meet her eyes. "You thought I'd abandoned you?"

"I thought of you as caught in the middle. But everyone else wants nothing to do with me."

"It's not like that. I think Mum and Dad got themselves stuck in a corner. Tara and her kids wouldn't ignore you."

"I'm sick of Tara or Shae fighting my battles with Mum and Dad."

"They haven't abandoned you. Maybe just meet them halfway?"

Charli lets me go. "You thought I was lucky two seconds ago?"

I huff and drop my face into my hands. "It's all just really fucked up."

Charli draws a circle on my back. "Shit. Sorry."

"Stop apologising. Everyone needs to stop friggin apologising to me."

"Ok, I will. Tell me, if you weren't studying law, what would you be doing?"

My mind is totally blank. Except that tumbleweed. "No idea. I'm so messed up."

"Stay with me and we will figure it out." She gets up. "I'll get the tea."

"Tea doesn't fix everything."

She looks over her shoulder and smirks. "It does way more than coffee."

I grin. "Coffee is life."

Keys jingle and the front door opens.

"Charlotte?" a smooth male's voice calls out.

Charli moves towards the front door, grinning. "Hey, you're back."

The guy, *whoah*, the really handsome guy, places a bag wafting of Chinese food on the kitchen bench. He kisses Charli on the lips. "Yeah, I came back sooner than expected." He notices me on the couch and surprise brightens his eyes. "Oh, hi there."

"Felix, this is my sister, Brittany," Charli says, gesturing towards me. "She's staying with us for a few days."

"Oh, cool. How are you, Brittany?" Felix asks with a wave.

I nod with a weak smile. "I'm ok."

Charli takes Felix's hand. "Are you ok with the couch? I want to stay close to Brittany."

He kisses her forehead. "Of course."

"I didn't know you had a boyfriend," I say.

The two laugh, dropping hands.

I squint at them. "What?"

"We aren't together like that," Felix says, taking a container out of the bag.

Charli edges towards me and whispers, "It's kinda like an open relationship type thing."

I gasp, wide-eyed. "What? How does that work?"

"Easy," Felix says, taking out the rest of the containers. "Neither of us want to be in shackles."

I look at Charli and smile out of shock. "Shackles?"

"Felix lives in Melbourne. When we travel, we crash with each other." She shrugs. "I don't have a great track record with relationships. We can't all be as lucky as you."

"Oh, what's this now?" Felix says, gathering plates and cutlery. "Brittany, I hope you like Chinese food."

"Love it," I reply.

"Brittany has been with her boyfriend since grade ten. They're the cutest thing ever."

"Wow, congratulations," Felix says.

I shrug. "It wasn't like we were together the entire time. Everyone has ups and downs."

"I'm surprised he's not here," Charli says, sitting beside me. "I'd figure he'd be glued to your side."

"He doesn't know what happened."

"What? How can that be?"

"I don't want him to know yet."

"You guys had a fight?"

I glance at the emerald promise ring on my finger. "No. We don't talk enough to fight."

"What does that mean? What's happening with you two?"

I shake my head. "Just drop it, Charli. I don't want to talk about it."

"Charlotte is a nosey-parker," Felix jokes, placing food on the coffee table. "Aren't you?"

Charli scoffs, "Whatever."

I eye Charli. "Makes sense you two aren't in a relationship. You hate being called Charlotte."

"No, Felix just likes given names. He never uses nicknames. Like, ever. No matter how close he is to a person."

"How very formal," I joke.

"I just like names," he says, dishing out the food. "How long are you visiting?"

"Ah, I dunno."

"She lives in Sydney," Charli says, mouth full of chicken and rice.

"Oh, I thought you must have come up from Charlotte's hometown."

I shake my head. "No, I live on campus."

Felix drops his chopsticks and whispers to Charli, "Oh, you told me about that right... how your parents..."

Charli munches more, nodding and looking down.

I look between them. "About how they cut her out?"

Charli *tsks*. "Brit, don't."

"What?"

"Just leave it."

I bite my lip and then sigh. "You think if I quit uni they'd stop talking to me too?"

Charli eyes me. "Are you thinking about dropping out?"

"Or changing subjects."

"Law sucks?"

I nod. "Law sucks."

Charli puffs a laugh and turns her attention back to her food.

"What would you change to?" Felix asks.

My mind is still as blank as always. It's like I'm unable to make a decision about my life. It's easier not to. It's easier to not exist.

"Just let her eat," Charli says.

Felix sits back. "Sorry, I didn't mean to be pushy."

"She has a lot on her mind."

Charli spies the bandage and I instinctively rub my wrist. It's itchy, and I unravel the bandage.

"Should you be taking that off already?" Charli asks.

"It's ok," I say as the stitches become visible.

"Oh, Brit," Charli hushes.

Felix leans over the coffee table. He exhales and then says, "You did that?"

My eyebrows lift and I nod.

"I have some of those," he says and lifts his sleeves to show insides of his forearms. I frown at all the scars. "Have you done your thighs? They were my place of choice throughout high school. They're easier to hide."

My back stiffens. "I'm not some crazy cutter."

Charli clutches my knee. "Brit, it's ok."

"I didn't mean to offend or accuse you of anything," he says. "I know what it's like to sink into a black hole with no exit." He nods at my wrist. "That's a dangerous place to cut."

My eyes prick as my mind fills with blood gushing out of the wound. I close my eyes hard to rid the images.

"It's not like it used to be, you know," Felix says, and I open my eyes. "Living with mental illness doesn't have to mean being alone."

I lean backwards, my lip upturning.

"Felix, no," Charli whispers, squeezing my knee. "She's not diagnosed."

Diagnosed? "I don't have a mental illness."

They stare at me with rounded eyes, pushing for something to say.

My eyes water. "Why are you looking at me like that?"

Charli forces a smile and strokes my arm. She's moments from sobbing.

"What?"

"It's ok," Felix says, scooting forward. "We can talk about it, if you want. I've been there."

"Been where?" I ask defensively.

"Brittany." Charli takes my hand. "Remember how Mum and Dad sent me to rehab when we were seventeen?"

"Yeah?"

"I didn't think there was anything wrong with me. I thought I shouldn't be there. I wasn't a junkie, and I didn't want to deal with losing Kellie." There's a catch in her voice. "But they kept talking to me, waiting for me to open up. Eventually I was diagnosed with depression."

"I didn't let anyone talk to me either," Felix says. "I was constantly hurting myself, but I wouldn't admit why. It's a hard road to take on your own. When it's so dark you can't see a way out." He nods to Charli. "But you have your sister, and she understands. She's been there."

I frown at Charli. "It's not the same thing."

She squeezes my hand. "You don't think you're still sad about being in that accident? Angry?"

I grit my teeth and look between them with foggy eyes. "I don't have depression."

"It's nothing to be ashamed of," Charli whispers. "Hell, your boyfriend has it. Why haven't you talked to him about this stuff?"

I throw her hand and groan. "Because he's trying to move past it. He doesn't want to be the guy with depression anymore. He's trying to be happy. Bryce deserves better than to be dragged down by me."

"Brit, he loves you."

I close my eyes tight, fighting back the tears.

"You were there for him when he was fighting through it. Of course he'd be there for you. Don't say you don't deserve him."

"You don't know," I whisper.

"Tell me about it then."

I groan and push off the couch. A pain radiates in my hip and I wince. I hold my hip and lean forward. Ouch.

Charli stands and presses on my back. "Sit back down."

I sit out of necessity and turn away from her. I want her to drop it.

Charli sighs and picks up her chopsticks. "Let's just eat."

Felix sits by Charli's legs. He rests his head against her knee as he presses the remote towards the TV.

I breathe out a small amount of relief.

A small spasm of tension camps between my shoulders.

Mental illness? They accused me of having depression? In my mind, I slam the door shut on the subject.

After dinner, Felix takes a shower, which leaves Charli and I alone on the couch. I curl up and watch her play with her long, straight brunette hair. She's out of her work uniform, and her tank top and shorts show off her arms and legs.

"How many tattoos do you have now?" I ask.

She smiles blissfully. "Eight."

I turn my head sideways. "What is the one on your foot?"

Charli's foot lifts in the air. "It's a compass."

My nose crinkles. "Why would you want that?"

"Because I travel."

"But it's not a working compass. It's not like it'll point you where you want to go."

She lowers her foot. "You don't know that. Maybe where my foot points is always the way I want to go." She turns the inside of her arm towards me. "This is my newest one. D'you like it?"

"Chinese symbols?"

"No, it's Japanese Kanji."

"You're not Japanese. How do you know it says the right thing?"

Charli flops her arm down. "Forget it."

"What is it supposed to say?"

"Nevermind. Forget about it."

I kick back on the couch. "Fine."

We sit in silence, staring at a TV show I guarantee neither of us are interested in. I look back at her. She sits upright with a bent knee to her chest, and plays with a lock of hair. Her face is strong and sure. There's so much confidence about her. Freedom. A life lived.

"I'm jealous."

She turns to me. "Huh?"

"Of you. I'm jealous of all you're travelling."

"You can travel too. You can do anything you want. Just decide what you want."

"Are you still going to help me find it?"

She swivels towards me. "I'll help you do absolutely anything. Just talk to me about it."

I lean against the couch armrest and gaze at the ceiling. "I never do anything."

"How do you mean?"

"I never go out or anything. Mum and Dad give me ten grand a semester and it's such a waste."

"*Pa-ha*, what?" Charli splutters.

I look at her. "Huh?"

"Ten grand? They gave you *ten grand*?"

"Each semester."

Her eyes bulge. "They've given you twenty grand?"

"It's for food, books, and whatever else I need. They'd give you the same if you went to uni."

Her mouth hangs open as she utters shock.

"But it's a mega waste. I never go out. The leftover money just sits there."

"How much?"

It's like there's a lightbulb shining over my head. "Enough

to go overseas."

"You want to go on a holiday?"

I clutch her wrist. "Come with me."

"I just got back from—"

"I have enough for the both of us," I interrupt. Excitement bubbles inside me. "We can go anywhere."

She stares at me with the same intensity I do her. "Where?"

"I literally don't care."

Her eyes wander the room as she ponders. "Bali?"

I shrug, smiling. "Sounds good."

"With your mind a jumble, we could go to a retreat. They have these great yoga and meditation retreats in the Ubud Mountains."

I grin. "Do they have cocktails?"

"We could stay at a resort instead."

"No, maybe you're right, a retreat is what I need."

"Are we really doing this? Going travelling together?"

I hug her like a life-preserver. "I'm ready to book it now."

She holds onto me tightly and murmurs, "They give you ten thousand dollars, but completely cut me off. Who the fuck does that?"

"I'm sorry. I thought you knew."

"It's not your fault. It's just irritating."

"Our parents are beyond irritating." I stroke her hair and smile. "I love using their money to escape with you."

Her shoulders jiggle as she laughs in my arms. "Imagine Dad's face."

I try my best Dad imitation. *"Now Brittany, that wasn't a*

wise thing to do."

Charli's loud laughter shakes both our bodies.

"When can we go?" I whisper.

"Few days?"

"Can't wait."

6

Charli

"Take something from my wardrobe to wear," I tell Brittany as I scoot out of bed at 10am. "Or you can live in that oversized t-shirt all day."

Brittany hugs her waist, smiling. "It's the comfiest thing I've ever worn."

I smirk, opening my wardrobe. "I know, it's my favourite PJ shirt."

Brittany giggles. "You shouldn't have let me borrow it. You're never getting it back."

I strip off my pyjamas and slip on a *Red Hot Chili Peppers* t-shirt and black shorts. I tug another t-shirt from the pile and toss it at Brittany. "And d'you want a skirt or jeans?"

Brittany lifts the t-shirt and her smile fades.

"What?" I ask. "Are you dissing my fashion sense already?"

She forces a smile and *tsks*. "Of course not." She pulls off my PJ shirt and slips on the t-shirt. She stares at her torso and then wraps the bedsheet around her.

"Brit? What is it?"

She sighs and slips out of bed. "Look," she says, pulling at the fabric clinging to her stomach.

Gulp. It's not meant to be a tight t-shirt. "What? It looks fine."

She deadpans me. "Don't give me that. I'm fat."

A surprised laugh puffs out of me. "As if. You're not fat."

She sits on the edge of the bed. "The only exercise I do is walking to classes. I'm not active. It's hard. Once I put on weight after the accident, it was ridiculously hard to get rid of it. Dancing was the only exercise I did before."

I plonk down beside her. "But you can exercise now, right? A light activity?"

She nods, and a frown draws her face. "I can. I just don't have the energy. I didn't care enough to start something."

I clasp her hand. "Could you start dancing again? Like, a beginner's class, maybe? To ease in?"

Her laugh is sarcastic. "I did. It was the living worst. I hated it. I was terrible. I was in a room full of amateurs and the worst one."

"You're being hard on yourself."

"I was auditioning to be a professional dancer." Fury lights her eyes. "Beginner's jazz won't cut it."

I eye the stitches zigzagging her wrist. Something cut her.

"I'll play hooky from work," I suggest. "What do you want to do? Retail therapy? Facials?"

"Lay on the couch and watch rom-coms?"

My lips curl. "Sure. We can do that."

"Got pants for me?"

"If we're having a movie day, we can stay in PJs."

"You have baggy shorts, right?"

"We can go to your dorm and get your clothes. You're still covering your stomach. You're obviously uncomfortable."

She chews her lower lip. "I hate being in your clothes."

I scoff, "You are dissing my fashion sense."

She sighs. "No. You're my identical twin, and your clothes are too skinny for me. It fucking sucks."

"If it helps, I'm too skinny for my own good."

"Nah-uh. You look great. You're a babe."

I kiss her cheek. "You're a babe."

She smirks and playfully pushes me away. "I can't go back to my dorm. I can't face my R.A.. Crap. What if she's blabbed to the whole hall?"

"Can we call Bryce? Does he have a key to your room?"

She shakes her head. "He can't know what happened."

"I thought he was your rock?"

"Just stop. I can't talk to him yet."

I drop it. I can tell by her eyes, she's adamant about keeping Bryce out of the loop.

"Let's do breakfast," I suggest. "Afterwards, I'll go to campus to get your stuff."

Her body relaxes. "Thanks, Sissy."

I've visited Brittany at university once. Appalling. My sister and I live in the same city and we never see each other. Granted, I travel a lot. When I am in Sydney, I work as many shifts as I can to pay for the next trip.

But there's no excuse to not book in twin-time.

I unlock the door to Brittany's dorm room and nudge it open.

"Oh Brit." The words tumble out slow and sad. I clasp a hand over my mouth as I step inside. I close the door and press my back against it. Sickness swirls in my stomach as my eyes follow the trails of blood. I swallow hard as my mouth waters with a disgusting taste. The dry blood is a maroon, almost navy colour.

I whip out my phone. I hate that I'm googling *how to clean up bloodstains.* I suck in air, hoping for bravery, and leave for a supermarket to get supplies.

When I'm in the dormitory hall, I lean against her doorframe. I didn't realise she was this unhappy. I didn't mean to ignore her. It wasn't like that. I was trying to pursue things I want out of life. I didn't realise she wasn't doing the same thing.

I gulp.

I didn't realise she wanted to end it all.

A tear escapes my eye as I croak a sob. I sniff and wipe my face quickly. *Get your shit together, Charli. We need to fix things for Brittany. No time for you to lose your shit.*

After a trip to the supermarket, I have trouble stopping myself heaving as I clean the floor. The industrial cleaning supplies are sending my head for a loop, but I can deal with the fumes more than the blood. I didn't think I had a weak stomach. Or is it just the fact it's my sister's blood? My poor sister who has already braved enough heartbreaking ordeals.

I dump a bucket of filthy cloths and water, and an almost empty liquid bottle in the dumpster outside the dorm. I pack a bag of Brittany's clothes, toiletries, makeup, and the perfume sitting on her desk.

"Charli?"

I recognise his voice instantly as I close Brittany's door. "Hey Bryce."

He eyes the door. "Is Brittany in there?"

"No," I draw it out.

"Do you know where she is?" his voice is small. "She hasn't responded to my calls or texts. It's not totally unusual for us to go days without seeing each other, but she usually replies by now."

"She's ok," I say quickly to reassure him. "She's at my place."

He steps closer to me. "Why is she at your place?"

I fidget. "Sisterly bonding?"

"Ok?"

He searches my face for cracks, so I force out the first story I can think up. "We're going on a road trip to Sanford. You know, like, try to have a peaceful time with our family."

"Really?" He half believes me. "Maybe I should visit Sanford too. I haven't seen Dad and Cait since the semester began."

"No, don't," I rush in my panic. "Just not at the same time as us, you know. We need to try really hard with our parents right now. Brit didn't want any distractions. Is that cool?"

"Is that why she's not talking to me?" Confusion coats his face. "She thinks I'm a distraction?"

"Did you guys have a fight?"

"No. Why? What did she say?"

"Nothing. Really."

We stare at each other in silence. I feel like he's not telling me something, and I'm definitely not telling him something. Imagine if he had come by when I was cleaning up the bloodstains. What would I have said then?

I bite inside my cheek. "Look, I really don't know." I hitch the bag over my shoulder and take a few steps backwards. "I'll get her to call you, ok."

He nods. "Ok. Thanks, Charli."

I smile as kindly as I can and move down the hall.

"I've booked us in!" Brittany cheers from the couch, my laptop perched on her lap. "We're on the plane in two days."

I sit her bag on the kitchen bench, and walk further into my apartment. "That's great. I got everything I could think of for you."

"That's all good. Once we're in Bali, I can buy new stuff. I'm due for a new wardrobe."

I edge towards her. "You seem to have perked up."

She grins. "I'm just so excited to go."

I sit on the armrest beside her. "I ran into Bryce."

She flinches. "At uni?"

"Outside your dorm room. He was asking where you are.

Why didn't you tell him you're here? Are you going to tell him you're leaving the country?"

She scoffs. "You make it sound so dramatic."

"Brit. Why are you avoiding him? He looked genuinely concerned and misses you like crazy."

She bats a hand. "He'll be fine."

"*Brittany*," I scold. "You're not being fair."

She lifts her arm, showing off the stitches. "Life's not fair."

I slip off the armrest and back away.

Brittany groans and slides the laptop onto the couch. "What did you say to him?"

"That you're staying with me and we're going back to Sanford to see our parents."

Her eyes round. "Why would you do that?"

"I panicked."

"He'll call Mum!"

"No, I told him to let us lay low."

She runs her hands over face. "I can't wait to be on that plane."

"You know, you could always talk to Shae," I suggest, tentatively. Her eyes shoot daggers. "She's a counsellor now. If you don't want to seek professional help, at least she'd have ways to help."

"Drop it. I don't want that kind of help."

"What about Nick? How often do you see him these days?"

"I haven't seen him in ages. I miss him, but I can't handle making him sad by telling him I'm not doing ok."

"He'd want to help," I urge. "We could visit him, if you

want."

She stares at the laptop screen. "I dunno."

"Want me to text him?"

She holds out her hand. "Pass my phone. I'll text him."

I smile and hand over the phone. My heart warms at her effort to hang out with someone. Yet, it doesn't come close to the fact she came to me first.

My hand slides over hers. "I'm really glad you came to me for help."

She lowers the phone and smiles. "You're the only person I truly trust."

"Oh, Brit."

"You've been through hell. At least you listen to me." She goes back to texting. "I didn't want to admit I was struggling. But it was better than staying silent."

Like you did with Bryce? I don't push it.

Brittany's phone pings. "Nick said he's hanging at his dorm and he's cool for us to meet up."

"Is that what you want?"

She bites her lip, her grip intense on the phone. "It'd be nice to see him." She looks me in the eyes. "D'you mind?"

"Of course not. I haven't seen Nick in ages."

"You two don't exactly get on."

I shake my head, averting my eyes. "We're fine. That was high school."

"Ok." She stands. "Lemme take a shower, then we can go?"

"Sure."

"Brittany!" Nick cheers, arms out wide, as he meets us outside his building at the Institute of Music where he attends school. He pulls Brittany into a hug and says into her hair, "It's so good to see you." He looks over her shoulder and smiles. "Hey Charli. How are ya?"

I nod and smile. "Good, thanks."

Brittany holds onto Nick and whispers, "I'm so glad to see you."

"You all right?" he asks, rubbing her back. "You sound a little down."

Brittany pulls out of the hug and fakes a laugh. "I guess you could say that."

His arms unravel her, and he notices her wrist. "What's this?"

I take a step closer. "Perhaps we should go inside first."

Nick swipes a white card by the glass doors, and they open. He shows us inside and says to Brittany, "Did you have an accident?"

"Yeah." As she answers, I edge closer by her side. Concern shapes Nick's face as he waits for her to elaborate.

"Is there somewhere we can sit?" I ask Nick. "Brit's been using her cane lately, so it'd be good if she didn't have to stand too long."

"Oh, shit. I'm sorry," he says to Brittany.

Brittany rolls her eyes. "I'm not a total hopeless case."

My shoulders bunch. "I'm just tryin to look out for ya."

She touches my arm. "It's ok."

Nick shows us to a common room and gestures to the sofas.

"Take a seat. It was great to hear from you, Brit. It's been too long." He turns to me and smiles. "You too, of course. I just meant the text was from Brittany."

"It's ok, Nick," I say, sitting beside Brittany. "Stop sweating."

He laughs and sits on the adjacent sofa. "So, what's been going on?"

Brittany plays with the material of her shirt. "Not much."

Brittany's fidgety awkwardness makes me tense. I try to lighten the mood and ask Nick, "How's school going?"

Nick's eyes widen as he takes a large breath in. "Good." He breathes out. "Good, but hectic. A lot of stuff on my plate, but I'm loving it. So can't complain."

"That's the most important thing," Brittany replies.

I pat her thigh and say, "Brit's not loving school right now."

Nick sits forward. "Oh, I'm sorry to hear that. Rob is always saying how proud he is of you. I got the impression you were enjoying it. You seemed to do really well."

Brittany recoils slightly. "Dad makes everything so hard. He and Mum tell me how proud I'm making them, but they never ask how I'm feeling."

His head tilts. "How are you feeling?"

She turns her wrists upwards. "Not good."

Nick points to the stitches. "What happened there?"

"It's a cut," she replies.

My stomach turns in on itself. Her room. The bloodstains.

Nick's jaw flexes, and his face grows pale. "How was it cut?"

Brittany looks at me and then at Nick. "By me."

"Oh, Brittany," Nick rushes, moving towards Brittany. He

kneels in front of her and clutches her knees. "Why? What has happened?"

"Nothing." She blinks. "Absolutely nothing. Nothing happens in my life. Nothing worth noting. Nothing worth continuing."

I grab onto her shoulder and squeeze. I shut my eyes tight to stop the watering. *Please, stop talking like this.*

"How can you say that?" he whispers. "You're a beautiful, strong, amazing woman. You deserve life." He looks at me and then back at Brittany. "*We* need you in our lives."

I nod, running my arm behind Brittany's back.

She lifts her wrist. "I regretted it immediately."

His lips ever so slightly curve up. "I'm glad."

"*Ohmigawd,*" a high-pitched voice enters the room. A tall, slender boy with bleach blond hair and fair skin, sashays his way into the common room. His arms lift in a cheer. "Are these the twins? Why hello, hello!"

"Ben," Nick starts, wiping under his eye as he stands. "Take it down a notch."

"What?" Ben says, lowering his arms. "You said you were excited to see them, therefore I'm acting excited."

Nick intertwines his fingers with Ben's, and says, "Read the room."

Ben looks over at us. "Yeah, there is a funeral vibe in here."

"*Ben,*" Nick hisses.

Ben gulps. "Aw, shit. Someone did die?"

Nick rolls his eyes. "No. Just cool it."

Brittany tilts her head as she watches the boys' hands.

"Nick, is this your boyfriend?"

Nick blows out a breath. "*Oops*, sorry, should totally do introductions. Brittany and Charli, this is my boyfriend Ben. Ben, my step-sisters."

Ben drops Nick's hand and slides down beside me. "Hey sisters. How are we doing? What can I do to turn those frowns upside-down?"

"You're very chipper," Brittany says, leaning forward to see Ben beside me.

"I'm the uplifting spirit in everyone's lives," Ben says cheerily, his arms twirling upwards.

"Translation, he's nosey," Nick says, sitting on the coffee table.

"Nosey? *Muah*?" Ben says, clutching his chest.

"Anyway," Nick says to Ben, "Brittany was telling me some stuff, and maybe it'd be better if it was just us to talk it over?"

Ben's eyebrow raises. "You're kicking me out of the *common* room?"

"It's ok," Brittany blurts. "He can stay, I don't mind."

"You sure?" I ask, rubbing her back. She couldn't talk in front of Felix, how is this going to go?

Nick eyes his boyfriend. "He can be a bit much."

"Ex-squeez-me," Ben replies. "I am nothing but loving and supportive."

Brittany sighs and flings her arm across my legs, turning her wrist up. "I did something stupid."

"Damn, girl," Ben says, lifting Brittany's hand. "What ya go and do that for?"

"Ben," Nick huffs.

"I dunno, it was dumb," Brittany says.

I take Brittany's hand from Ben and fold her arm around mine.

"It's not dumb," Ben says. "If you were that sad, it can't be helped." He points to himself. "Think this queen didn't get the shit kicked out of him? We all have dark moments."

I look at Brit, and she shows a weak smile. "Thanks."

Ben jumps up and slings his hands in the pockets of his black skinny jeans. "Wanna feel better?"

"What do you mean?" I ask.

"Nick and I are hitting the clubs tonight. You ladies should join."

Nick stands. "I think I'll pass tonight."

"As if." Ben whacks Nick's arm. "You're so coming."

Brittany shuffles forward on the sofa. "I'll go."

I raise an eyebrow. "Clubbing?"

She shrugs. "Why not?"

"You're dealing with a lot right now."

"We can take you," Nick offers.

Ben points at me. "And you're coming too."

I point to Brittany. "Only to watch her."

Ben throws an arm around Nick's shoulders, and says, "Perfect, it's settled then. We will hit the clubs tonight as a foursome."

"Are you sure you want to go clubbing?" I ask Brittany.

"I'm dying to have some fun," she replies.

I clasp her hand and an uneasy feeling washes through me.

Staring at her stitched wrist, I am worried clubbing is the last thing this girl needs. My mind wanders back to seventeen-year-old me who needed clubs, alcohol and drugs to hide my feelings. But Brittany has her sister to hold her up.

I promise to not let anything else bad happen to this beautiful girl.

7

Brittany

"*Ohmigawd*, Brittany!" Madison squeals as Charli and I walk towards the club.

"Madi!" I cheer as she wraps her arms around me.

"When Nick said he was going out with you guys tonight, there was no way I was gonna miss out," Madi says with giddiness. "It's been ages since we've hung out. How come I never see you?"

"Ah, I dunno." I stumble on the words, because I seriously don't have an answer.

"Oh, hey Charli," Madi says as we pull out of the hug. She laughs and adds, "Sorry, didn't mean to ignore you."

Charli swats a hand. "Don't mention it."

I can tell Charli's not concentrating on Madi. She has been

watching me like a hawk since we left Nick's. She's worried about me going out tonight. As we got dressed and applied our makeup, she kept asking me if I was sure I wanted to do this.

For the millionth time, yes!

I've spent the last year cocooned. Just let me be a freakin butterfly!

"You two look so pretty," Nick says, stepping beside Madi. He leans in and kisses my cheek. "You seem to have perked up, Brit."

"Let's get to the bar," I say with a grin.

"You wanna get drunk?" Madi asks.

I clutch her shoulders. "Desperately."

Madi links arms with me and pulls me towards the entrance of the club. Out of the corner of my eye, Charli jerks forward, ready to pull me back. But she backs off.

Thank goodness.

"Welcome ladies," Ben calls, posing beside the club's bouncer. He waves us in, saying, "We get to cut in line. Yes, you can thank me by buying me a drink."

"Have you been here before?" Madi almost shouts in my ear as we enter the club. The music is pounding.

"No, never," I reply.

"We come here all the time," Madi says, grinning ear-to-ear. "The boys love it." She looks over her shoulder. "Charli, you been here before?"

Charli nods. "A few times. This girl I was seeing liked it."

Madi stops dead, throwing an arm out to catch Charli mid-step. "Ex-squeez-me? A girl? You're gay?"

Charli chews her lip, eyes darting for an answer. "No. I don't label myself."

"You just got a million times more interesting to me," Madison says, looking Charli up and down.

I tug Madi's hand. "Bar please. And she's bi."

Charli grumbles behind me. I don't get why she hates the label. She is bi... isn't she?

Madi swivels around and clasps my hand on the way to the bar. "Since when? Not high school, because how did I not know?"

I smirk. "Because the fact she was on drugs was more distracting."

A set of hands land on my shoulders, and as I look to my side, Nick slides close to me.

I smile sweetly at him. "Hey."

"Hey. What can I get you to drink?" he asks.

"Do they do any crazy cocktails here?"

He gazes around the bar. "I dunno. Let's get a hot bartender and ask him what the craziest thing he's got is."

Madi laughs boisterously. "Be careful. You may get more than you bargained for."

I pan across the array of hunky bartenders. All sport sparkly bow ties, silver suspenders, and shirtless six-pack abs.

A smirk plays at Nick's lips.

I laugh and ask, "Maybe you're betting on seeing more."

He nudges me. "As if you're not too."

Madi shooshes him, tapping a finger to her lips. "Careful, boyfriend incoming," she teases.

"So, twins," Ben announces, slinging an arm around Charli

and me. "What do ya think of the place?"

"Charli's already been here," Madi blurts. She whacks an arm at Nick, saying, "Did you know she dates girls?"

"Huh?" Nick questions, taken aback.

"*Ohmigawd*," Ben cheers, leaning into Charli. "Sorry, hunny, didn't realise you were one of us. *Gee*, didn't get a gay vibe from you."

If you opened a dictionary to the word discomfort, it would be a picture of Charli's face at this exact moment.

Nick pulls his boyfriend towards himself. "Ben, lay off her."

"What?" Ben questions defensively.

"You're too much. Let them ease into getting to know you," Nick tells.

Ben kisses Nick, wrapping his arms around his neck. "Sorry, Babe. Are you getting me a drink?"

An easy smile dashes across Nick's lips, and his hands clasp around Ben's waist. "Vodka Redbull?" Nick asks.

Ben kisses Nick's cheek. "Yes, please."

"And we gotta find something *over-the-top* for Brittany to drink," Nick says, shooting me a wink.

Charli clutches my wrist. "Speaking of easing in," she utters. "Maybe you wanna rethink drinking tonight."

I groan and roll my eyes. "I, like, never drink. It'll be fine."

"That only means you'll get even more plastered," Charli argues.

"Darl, you gotta lighten up," Ben says, tugging on Charli's arm. "C'mon, we're dancing."

"Huh?" Charli blurts. "Nah, I'm good. My sis—"

He tugs until she's forced to follow. "Nah, darl, it's not optional."

Ben wraps Charli in his arms on the dancefloor and spins her in fast circles. Dizzy and with a huge grin, Charli seems to have taken her worries off me. For one moment, at least.

I nudge Nick, and say, "So, your boyfriend is really..."

"Gay?" he jokes.

Laughter sizzles out of both of us.

"I just mean, I didn't pick you to be with someone so, *extroverted.*"

"Me either. But Ben is hard to ignore."

"That he is. Is everything ok with you two? That thing Madi said earlier about being careful not to say anything because Ben was coming over..."

Nick shakes his head, and I notice his eyes roll. "Nah, it's all good. He just gets weirdly jealous about the dumbest stuff."

"Ouch. That would be tough to deal with."

"What about you and Bryce? You didn't want to bring him tonight?"

I pick at my fingernail to avoid the question.

"Brit?"

"I dunno. Like, um, we're good. Just... a rut, I guess."

He nods like he understands, or is at least trying to. "You guys have been together forever, so I guess that's normal."

"Yeah, totally."

Nick orders our group's drinks, and we laugh at Madi making friends with a random group of guys further down the bar.

"Hey, how's Reece doing?" Nick asks, passing me a drink.

"Good. I think. I saw him on campus, but didn't chat because he was on the way to class."

"I haven't spoken to him in ages."

"How come?"

I sip on the drink. It's lime green colour with an arrangement of extravagant garnishes. A sour apple taste glides over my tongue, and a dizzy signal fires in my brain. *Yum.*

"I could ask you the same thing," Nick says. "Nice drink?"

"Yes," I say with a smile. I jitter at the thought of not talking with any friends in too long. "Sometimes it feels awkward. After high school, it's like we all went off towards different lives, and I don't know how to keep in contact with everyone. I don't want to slow anyone down, or bore anyone."

Nick slings an arm around me. "You're not boring. I always have fun with you."

"I don't feel fun these days."

"You need to change that. You deserve fun in your life."

Warmth wriggles from my heart and spreads through my chest. "I am. Charli and I are hopping on a plane to Bali. *Shoosh.* Don't tell Dad."

"That's awesome." He lifts his vodka Redbull to his lips. "Why the secret?"

"I just don't want my parents' judgement right now. I have a lot to figure out."

He takes a big sip of his drink and then sets the glass on a table. "Well, I won't say anything. Just promise to keep me in the loop."

I cuddle close to him. "I promise."

"Wanna dance?" he asks.

Nick's smile is so *uber* adorable. How could I say no?

I clutch his hand. "Lead the way."

Nick and I shuffle our way onto the dancefloor. I lift my cocktail glass high, and we make our way close to Charli and Ben.

"See, darl," Ben cheers over the music. "Your sis is fine."

Charli laughs in frustration. "Can you lay off with the *darls*?"

Ben smirks. "I call everyone who needs to lighten up, darl."

I giggle as Charli's eyes slit as she stares at Ben.

"Lighten up?" she questions.

"You know it, darl. You seem uptight."

"Me? Uptight? Really?"

"Ya-huh."

Nick laughs as he hugs me. "Would you two knock it off?"

I lean into Nick as we dance. Tonight, I want to forget my life. I want to forget the problems, the decisions, and the pain. I watch the sparkle in Nick's dark brown eyes, and smile as big as he does.

The sour apple cocktail went straight to my head. Madi was quick to ensure I had another drink to replace it. I think the one I'm holding now is my third. Oh, *geez*, it could be the fourth? Ah, I dunno. Who cares? I can't think straight, and that's so much easier.

Ha!

I look around at all the hot gay guys dancing on the platforms, and giggle at myself for not thinking straight.

Wow. Can I just stay here forever? This is so much easier than everyday life. It's so much more fun. Why don't I go out more?

I look around for Madi and Nick, and it dawns on me... They never ask me to hang out. I'm here because I visited Nick after a really dark turn. Without doing that, I wouldn't be here. They'd be out without me. Having fun without me. Going on with their lives without a second thought about Brittany.

That's why I'm alone. No one cares.

Even my boyfriend prefers it when I stay home from parties. It's more fun that way. I'm a drag.

"Hey," Charli's voice booms beside me. She grasps my arm. "I lost you for a moment there. Stay close, ok?"

I nod and let her lead me towards a cocktail table. Ahead of us, I spy Nick at a bar. He's talking with a guy I don't recognise. They are laughing about something. Sounds about right, I'm not involved.

The guy moves away from Nick. As Nick leans against the bar, Ben storms towards him.

"What was that?" Ben asks Nick, accusingly.

Nick lifts his chin, somewhat recoiling. "What?"

"I just saw that guy sniffing around you," Ben says, hands gripping his hips, his head tilting from side-to-side. "What was that all about?"

Nick's nose scrunches. "What are you talking about? We were just talking."

Ben stomps a foot, huffing. "He was like, obviously into you."

Nick lifts his palm in front of Ben and slips past him. "Whatever."

I nudge Charli and nod my head at the boys. "Lovers' quarrel, or what? Do you think Nick is ok?"

Charli links arms with me. "Maybe we'll leave them to it for now. How are you doing? Are you ok being here?"

"Yeah. Why?"

"No, nothing. I was just checking, because a few days ago you were—"

My groan reverberates throughout my entire body. "Stop bringing it up."

"What? I'm sorry," she squeaks. "I didn't mean to upset you, or anything. I'm just worried about you."

I lean into her, grinning with appreciation. "Thank you, but tonight, can you forget it happened? I kinda wanna get smashed."

Charli sighs. "If you must drink, promise to stay close to me. I don't want you out of my sight."

I squeeze her cheeks and giggle. "Get me a vodka raspberry."

"At least your mood is up," she says with a hesitant smile.

"Yes. Get happy with me."

"Booze is a happiness mask," Charli warns. "It disappears."

I grit my teeth and frown as I stare into her grey eyes.

"What? I'm not wrong," she argues.

"Stop being a buzzkill."

"Dancefloor?" she offers.

I point behind her, frowning. "Bar."

Charli's eyes roll, and she takes my hand. She leads me to the bar, and I feel queasy about winning this argument.

My vision is cloudy. I'm like a vice-grip on Charli's hand. Walking into her apartment is like wading through sand.

Why is it so hard to walk?

Oh right, drunk.

"Bathroom?" Charli asks, holding me upright.

"Bed," I slur.

I feel light as a feather, but Charli's acting like I weigh ten tons. *Drama queen.*

Oof.

I faceplant the bed.

"You don't wanna change?" Charli asks, reefing the covers out from under me. "At least take your shoes off?"

"*Shoosh.* Drunk," I garble.

A throbbing pulsates inside my forehead. *Ohmigawd.* Is the bed spinning?

After a lot of racket, Charli gets into bed beside me.

"Why won't you talk to Bryce?" Charli whispers, as she wraps the heavy quilt around us.

I pull the blanket to my chin and scrunch my eyes shut.

"Something must have happened?" she digs. "Did he say something hurtful to you?"

"Just stop."

It comes out much more desperate than I meant. And now all I can think about is how much I want to suppress these sobs. But they roll out, one after the other, shaking my body like there's an earthquake inside me.

"I'm sorry," she whispers. "I'm so glad you want to be with me. I'm just surprised you don't want to be with him."

"Don't ask me," I sob.

Because I don't have a good answer.

Charli holds me like the anchor I need. Her body is rigid yet calming. She's a rock. I'm never letting her go.

8

Charli

"Here's a coffee," I say to Brittany, meeting her back at our terminal gate, paper coffee cup in each hand.

"Which one?" she asks groggily, sunglasses still over her eyes.

"They're both the same."

Brittany dips her glasses. "You're kidding. Since when do you drink coffee?"

"Since Cambodia," I say, sitting beside her. "They had black tea at camp, but no green. The coffee had more kick, and I needed all the help I could get on that trip."

She takes a cup and nudges me. "Looks like you could use a lot of help now. Looking a bit seedy, Sis."

"*Pa-ha*! Like you're one to talk, Hangover Sally."

"That's not even a saying."

"Doesn't make it any less true."

She sniggers, "Shuddup."

As I rub the headache from my temples, I check the display over the gate check-in. "How long til we board?"

"They should start in ten minutes." Brittany rests her coffee cup on the seat and stands up. "I'm going to the bathroom."

"Why do you always leave it to the last minute?"

Her eyes roll. "It's hardly last minute. They take ten years to check everyone in."

As she wanders away, I look at my phone. All night I toyed with sending this message. She keeps telling me no, but surely she wants him to know.

He should know.

I open my phone to messages.

She'll thank me later.

I text Bryce:

> **Brittany and I are boarding a plane to Bali. I don't know why she hasn't told you. You deserve to know where she is. She's fine, but working through some issues. We will have some sister time, and I'll keep you posted. Please try not to worry about her. I'll keep her safe.**

I slip the phone into my pocket and take a long sip of coffee.

She'll thank me later.

When Brittany walks back from the bathroom, I feel my pocket vibrate. I gulp and don't touch it.

Please don't worry, Bryce.

We board the plane and the business class air hostess is *uber* nice. Since leaving high school, I've been taking economy flights. It hasn't worried me. I travel for the destination, not the comfort level getting there.

On our family holidays, Mum and Dad always splurged on the very best. Brittany isn't in the mood to give that up. She booked two of the very best seats on the plane. It is with Mum and Dad's money, after all.

I hang my headphones around my neck and Brittany asks, "What movie are you gonna watch?"

"I'll see what they have in the documentary section."

She grimaces. "*Ick.* Really?"

I laugh at her judgement. "Yes. What's wrong with that?"

She flicks through the movie selection. "And who says Charlotte Jane doesn't know how to live?"

"Lemme guess. A rom-com where the girl dates a dickhead and then realises her best friend was her true love all along."

Brittany grins. "It's a classic."

I laugh again and flick the headphones over my ears, ready to glide through the next five hours of our flight.

After our flight, we take a shuttle to the resort hosting our yoga retreat. The roads fill with chaotic, horn-happy cars, vans, and motorcycles. We went to Bali a few times on family vacations. I've been here twice on my own, and every time it's hard to look out the window when driving through the cities. My stomach somersaults and my head gets dizzy. Not that I'd be missing much. The cities fill with malls, grubby streets, and crowds.

Give me the mountains any day!

As our shuttle creeps into the Ubud Mountains, I instantly feel at peace. The pleasant rainforest smell, the shade of tall trees, and the removal of tourist hordes.

The driver stops outside our small resort and helps us with our bags. Brittany's eyebrows arch, and I notice the way her nose slightly tilts up as we enter the retreat. I guess she didn't expect it to be quite as rustic. She booked a place I've been to before. It's quaint and non-superficial.

"You look like Mum right now," I tease.

Her face screws up. "What?"

I cup a hand over my mouth as I laugh.

"*Charli*," she hisses, horrified.

"You have her judgemental face on."

Brittany huffs and shifts her weight as her eyes pan the reception room. It's a small bamboo room, with a scattering of plants rich in jasmine and frangipani scent, a small wooden desk, and two cheerful Balinese women ready to greet us.

"I am judging it because it's my first time here," Brittany rationalises. "I'm allowed, aren't I?"

"Sure, *Julie*." I can't help continuing the teasing.

She gasps, affronted, and whacks my arm.

I laugh and move to the reception desk. "Hi ladies, we're Brittany and Charli Matthews."

"Welcome," they say at once, with bright grins and plump cheeks that make me instantly miss Sophia.

Walking through the resort, I feel at home. This is my kinda place. I wish back-to-back trips like this filled my life. I adore the physical work I do on volunteer trips, and I never want to give it up. Ah man, there's nothing like the serenity of getting in touch with nature and surrounding yourself with like-minded people who spread positive vibes.

I guess it reminds me of my time in rehab. Once I acknowledged I needed help and put the work in, I enjoyed the pursuit of feeling better. I hope Brittany gets a taste of that this trip. To open her mind to a life outside the norm. A way to live outside our parents' guidelines. To find happiness.

"What makes you go on trips like this?" Brittany asks as a hotel attendant shows us to our room.

"How calming the lifestyle is. The lack of responsibilities."

"Do you even have responsibilities back home?"

"My life in Sydney is hectic." I exhale hard. "All I do is work. I work to repay the money I spent on the trip. I work to save for the next trip. I spend hours raising money for the projects I volunteer on. I still go out to bars and go on dates. Then I feel guilty for spending money on my personal life."

"Oh."

I clutch her hand and smile to lift the mood. "We are here and we can forget our problems. You'll love it, I promise."

"I'll give you money for the work you're missing," Brittany offers.

"No, you don't have to. That's your money."

"Just tell me how much, and I'll transfer it to your bank account."

"That's really sweet of you."

"You came on this trip with me without hesitation. It's the least I can do."

"You're already bankrolling the trip."

She grins. "Nah. Mum and Dad are. They just don't know it yet."

Has my travel been selfish? I don't care about my job. Once again, I left when I felt like it. Granted, this is to spend time with my sister… as if my boss cares. My life is carefree. It's a series of events where I don't care about anything except how I feel in the moment.

I mean, what is my direction? I fly from place to place. I resist settling anywhere. I have my apartment in Sydney, but I avoid staying there for extended periods of time. I choose work, a club, or a date's place.

I avoid finding a future career path. Do I really want to be a bartender for the foreseeable future? No, I don't think so. I love the people I work with and how easy the shifts are. But I hate how the clientele look down their noses at me because I'm the server. I hate the classism that surrounds me when I'm in Sydney. Yes, it's in the underdeveloped nations I visit also, but I am with an organised group who free themselves from judgemental thoughts and purely want to help people. I want to be around those kinds of people full time.

Ah, I just don't know how.

"Here we are," the attendant says, opening a door.

I follow Brittany in and watch her gaze around the airy room. It's small, yet the breeze from the open balcony door creates space with the surplus of fresh air.

"Cute," she says, plonking on one of the single beds.

I thank the attendant and sit on the other bed across from

Brittany. "I'm so glad I'm here with you," I say.

She smiles and nods. "Me too."

"Even if it's not as upmarket as you expected?"

"It's a shake up to my everyday life, so that makes it a ten out of ten."

"That's awesome. I'm going to take a quick shower."

"Ok. I'm gonna check out the view."

As Brittany moves to the balcony, I check my phone. Bryce has responded to my text, but I didn't want Brittany to see it. I take the phone into the bathroom with me to respond.

"Do you remember the trip to Fiji we took before you went to Spain?" Brittany asks, lying backwards on her bed when I return from the shower.

I snort a laugh while towel drying my hair. "You mean the trip where you tried to pimp me out?"

A laugh wriggles her body. "Yeah, that one. Being in Bali kinda reminds me of that. The nice weather, far from home, doing activities with just you."

I toss the towel on the foot of the bed and comb my fingers through my damp hair. "That was a good trip. Especially after such a shitty year. Who'd have known the following year could be so much worse?"

"Yeah." She rolls onto her stomach. "It was a bit shit. Can I ask you a question?"

"Shoot."

"Why do you keep the dark colour in your hair?"

"What would you prefer me to dye it to?"

"Nothing. I'm surprised you dye it all."

"I've dyed it for years."

"Yeah. Why have you kept it dark for so many years?"

I shrug and stand in front of the floor-length mirror. "I like it. Don't you think it suits me?"

"It looks fine." Her hands nestle under her chin. "Along with your tattoos. Are you trying to look as much unlike me as possible?"

My mouth hangs ajar. "Not at all. Do you care people can now easily tell us apart?"

"Nah. People could always tell us apart. We've never dressed the same."

"Why don't you dye your hair anymore?" I ask her reflection. "And you rarely do your makeup these days."

She sits, and her eyes run the length of my hair. "There's a lot of stuff I can't be bothered with. It was the last thing I felt like doing after the accident. As the years went on, I stopped feeling the need for it. It's hard to care about the outside when the inside is messed up." I turn to face her as she adds, "Did you change your outside to make your insides feel better?"

"The first time I dyed my hair was the first time I felt like me. I'd accepted losing Kellie and was re-inventing myself. Kellie always told me to be real, not a fake Charli. I think I'm continually morphing into the real me."

Brittany smirks. "The real you is a brunette?"

"No, it's a symbol. I changed my hair when I changed my life. Maybe it's become a security blanket. Like, if I go back to blonde, I'll go back to old habits."

Brittany's expression drops. "That's probably the same with me and hair and makeup. If I do it again, I'll have to claim my life back."

I look at her sideways. "What are you hiding from?"

"It was so much work, looking a certain way to fit in. Not to mention, I was in great shape then. With my scars, my limp, and my inactivity, I couldn't see a way to fit back in."

"But it didn't stop you from making new friends at high school." I lower to the bed. "What stopped you from making friends at university?"

"Maybe I was scared to have the same friends as Bryce."

"Because it could be Chloe & Co 2.0?"

She swallows uncomfortably and nods.

My phone pings from the bathroom vanity. I move to pick it up.

(Bryce) Make sure she gets some fun, sun, and relaxes.

I text a quick **no worries**, and then hold the phone to my chest and smile as I walk back toward the twin beds.

"Who's that?" Brit asks.

I slip the phone into the waistband of my leggings. "Just a guy from work."

"You were smiling. Is this a romantic entanglement?"

I snort. "No, not at all." I eye her, ready to decode her body language. "What about your romance? Have you texted Bryce yet?"

She swings her legs off the bed and busies herself by tying

up her hair.

"Brit?"

"No, ok."

"Why not?"

She huffs. "I thought you'd promised to drop it."

"Fine," I sigh.

"I looked through the itinerary while you were in the shower," Brittany says, tapping a piece of paper on the desk. "There's a yoga class in about twenty minutes."

"You're keen?"

"Yeah, it'll be good to move after the flight." Brittany stands and smooths down her t-shirt. "Shall we get our yoga on?"

I smile at her attempt for enthusiasm and hitch a water bottle under my arm. "Let's do it. We can get dinner afterwards."

We roll our yoga mats across the woven bamboo flooring. I toss off my tank top to practice in my sports bra. I hate when my shirt billows out during yoga.

Brittany grimaces. "*Ugh*, put your shirt back on."

"What?" I gasp, slapping a hand over the roses tattooed on my ribs.

Brittany laughs. "Not that." She points to my stomach. "Look at your friggin four-pack. I can't look at that."

I sit cross-legged on my mat. "Shuddup."

She pokes at her stomach. "I used to have a tight core like that."

"I only got it because I lug supplies around a construction site."

She squeezes her stomach. "I only got this flab from sitting on my arse in lecture halls."

I whack her hand. "Stop it. You don't look bad."

Brit smirks. "But I don't look great."

"Brittany, we're here for a recharge, not to keep negative thoughts circling in our heads."

She pokes out her tongue and stretches her legs out on the mat.

Our instructor introduces herself as Hazel and explains we will meet two other yogis and one exceptional meditation specialist.

Brittany shoots me an uneasy glance.

"Meditation?" she whispers hesitantly.

"*Shoosh.* You'll love it. I promise."

Brittany wrinkles her nose and swats a hand at me, turning her attention back to Hazel.

Hazel eases us in with light breathing exercises and gentle stretches. Once we move into more repetitious stretches, I notice Brittany's stamina falter.

As she struggles with her stance in mountain pose, I whisper, "Does it feel hard after the plane ride? I know I don't feel all that together."

"*Shoosh* it. I'm trying not to fall."

"*Oops.* Sorry."

During downward dog, she huffs and groans, pushing out her calves and feet to find the right balance.

"It doesn't have to be perfect," I whisper. "Any attempt is a success."

She groans. "Shut it."

During floor work, I pull back my efforts. I don't want her watching me and comparing herself. I wish she could switch off, focus on her breath, and clear her mind.

Ha!

I'm one to talk. Here I am, fixating on how my sister should act, instead of concentrating on my mood and thoughts. *Hypocrite much, Charli?*

I shake out of my thoughts and concentrate on the instructor. Maybe Brittany can follow my example. Maybe I should stop trying to control how she feels and let her enjoy the new experience.

I need to back off and let her make up her own mind.

9

Brittany

Meditation sucks. I squint my eyes open and take in Charli's perfect posture as she sits cross-legged with the back of her palms resting on her knees. Her eyes are gently closed and her chest rises with relaxed breaths. She makes this look easy. She makes this look peaceful. Like it's not the most boring thing ever.

The instructor says to clear your mind. To forget all your troubles. To let them all melt away.

Fat chance.

It felt kind of nice when she was instructing us on how to breathe. In and out, in and out. But I've lost the plot now. It was nice having her voice to concentrate on. It kinda took me out of my head for a moment.

I lift an eyelid to spy on Charli. How is she doing this? I

watch her chest. She's got the *in-and-out* thing down.

I close my eyes and try again. In and out, in and out. I wonder how Bryce is at home. I really hope he hasn't called my mum or gone back to Sanford. *Gah*, I've lost the breathing already.

Meditation sucks.

I open my eyes and look over at Charli. I'm so over this.

I hate yoga. I hate how good my sister is at yoga. She's *uber* flexible. She's incredibly strong. She's amazing. I'm jealous. But I'm glad she's my sister. I'm glad I have someone like her looking out for me.

"How are you so good at this?" I ask as we return our mats.

"I do a lot of yoga," she says, playing with her much-too-long ponytail.

"Every day?"

"No, not every day. There's nothing I can stick at every day."

"Well, that's just annoying then."

"How's that?"

"If you did it every morning, it'd be easier to accept how much better you are."

Charli laughs as she skips down the stairs towards the gardens. "You don't do yoga, Brit, so how'd you expect to be better than me?"

"Remember in high school when I was better than you at most things?"

She scoffs and flops backwards onto the grass. "You were so annoying, you didn't even have to try. You kicked my butt at maths, you took one photo and it did better than all mine combined, and now you're studying law and are apparently taking it all in amazingly."

I lower myself to the ground. "Yet I don't care about any of those things."

"Do you think you would have auditioned for dance companies after high school if you didn't have an injury?"

"I would have liked to, but Mum and Dad would have probably talked me out of it."

"Maybe they'd be cool with it. Look at Dad when Nick left school to record music. He said Nick was pursuing his dreams so he let him go."

"But you're pursuing your dreams and they aren't happy with you."

"If I was organising the charity projects, maybe they'd care. I think it's the fact I'm a volunteer they don't like."

"That's so messed up."

Charli yawns and stretches her arms above her head. "That's our parents for ya."

"Charli, I'm not loving this whole *looking-for-Zen* thing."

She sits up. "Whaddaya mean?"

I get up off the grass and move closer to the swimming pool. Charli follows me and we sit by the edge, dangling our legs into the water. The nearby bar plays lo-fi hip hop and my shoulders do an unintentional bop along with the music.

"Talk to me," Charli insists.

I lean back and feel the sun warm my chest. "I'm not really into this yoga-meditation stuff."

"It's only been three days."

"Shouldn't I like it by now?"

"I won't force you to stick it out. Would you prefer to miss the classes and hang by the pool instead?"

I look down at the water and swing my legs. "Hmm, maybe."

"You haven't even swum yet. What's that about?"

I shrug. "Don't feel like it."

"Every resort we've ever been to you've been in the water every day."

"I didn't bring a swimsuit. Maybe I can go shopping instead of going to the next class."

She nods. "If that's what you want to do."

My feet make ripples in the water. "That's if I want a swimsuit."

"What's going on?"

"I've always worn bikinis."

"Me too."

"I would look shit in a bikini."

"As if."

I rub my stomach. "Well, I think I look shit in a bikini."

"You want to buy a one-piece?"

"It seems like I'm acting like an old person if I wear a one-piece."

"So, what do you want?"

I watch the sun reflect on the water. I look down at my activewear and say, "No one would see my body if I got in the water."

"No one cares what you look like."

I glare at her. "I care."

She nods. "Ok. Valid."

I sigh and pull at the clinging fabric of my leggings. "It's not just the extra weight, it's the scars. They run along my leg and on my hip, and they run onto my torso. I don't like looking at them. I don't want anyone to look and get disgusted."

"You have scars because you were in a car accident. We should just announce it. No one would care."

"Don't you dare."

"I'll announce I was a teenage drug addict. They'll judge me way harder than you."

"Would you *shoosh*?"

"No one cares, Brit. You need to stop caring what random strangers think. There's no negativity here. Use this place to let loose and have some fun."

I grizzle under my breath, "Whatever ya reckon."

Charli stands and holds a hand out to me. "Get up and dance with me."

"Are you nuts?"

Charli twists her hips and dips low on her knees.

"Hmm," I say with a nod. "You've got pretty good rhythm."

"See," Charli says, grabbing my arm. "The fact you say that, means you still know how to dance. It's in-built inside you."

I shake out my limbs as I stand beside her. "Uh, if it shuts you up."

I smile back at her and move with the beat. My moves are cautious yet fun. It feels good, moving intuitively to the music. Freely and without care, my arms pop, my head sways, my hips shimmy, and I bounce my knees.

A group of girls by the pool cheer and stand. They move closer to us, dancing in their group of four.

Charli giggles, her grin expansive. "You're captivating, Brittany May. Your energy brings the party."

I shimmy in a circle and mutter, "Whatever."

"I'm serious. Stop shutting the world out. The world needs your vibrancy."

I smile from the sheer joy of moving my body. The slow and graceful movements of yoga haven't called to me. The free and spontaneousness of dance has awakened me. I look across at the girls who joined in dancing and wish we were letting our hair down at a beach party or energetic club scene.

After building a small sweat from the impromptu dance, I wipe my brow and one phrase comes to mind. *Fuck it.*

With disregard, I slip into the pool. Under the water, the music and cheers muffle. Bubbles of air float from my mouth and lift above my eye line. I glide to the surface and emerge as Charli jumps into the pool.

"I decided I wanted in," I explain, happiness keeping me buoyant.

"Nice choice," she says, wading beside me.

I push myself backward and float on the water. I close my eyes and smile.

My top rides up on my stomach. As it balloons out, discomfort seizes me again. I pull down my shirt, and when it gets unbearable, I stand in the water.

I take as much time as I can, attempting enjoyment. Deep

down, I know I want to have fun here. When I'm tired of trying, I suggest to Charli we get food.

"Do you want to go back home?" Charli asks as we sit down to dinner.

"What? No?"

"But you hate it here."

I huff a sigh. "I don't hate it. It's just not my thing. I like being in Bali, but it's not like our family holidays."

"I thought you would like it because it's tranquil. But maybe you miss the commercialism."

"I miss what?"

"You prefer the *drop-of-a-hat* service and the shops lining every street."

"Yeah, I like that stuff."

"That's no problem. We can go to another area. It's no issue to leave the retreat early."

I tap my water glass, twisting my lips.

"What?" Charli deadpans.

I tap the glass harder.

"Tell me."

I lower my hand to the tabletop and sigh. "I have more money."

"Huh?"

"I have money we can blow." I crack a smile. "Remember how jealous I was when you went to Paris during your exchange?"

She smiles as surprise takes over her face. "Paris?"

I pick up my phone and wave it. "I can book flights and accommodation."

Charli laughs, shaking her head. "You want to go to Paris? Now?"

"Why not? We're practically halfway."

"You really have flicked the switch to impulsive."

"I still use Mum's travel agent. She can transfer everything and organise the new flights."

"What if it gets back to Mum?"

I wiggle my eyebrows. "Guess how many fucks I give about that?"

Charli throws her head back with laughter.

She looks at me, grinning. "Ok, let's do it."

I grin so wide my cheeks hurt. "Really?"

She nods, her smile just as big. "Really."

"Oh yay," I say, unlocking my phone. "I wanna book as close to the Eiffel Tower as I can."

"You know the French hate that thing."

"*Shoosh.* Don't ruin the magic for me."

She giggles. "Ok, sorry."

Walking along the Champs-Élysées, the most famous shopping precinct in the world, a fire alights in my chest. Awakening my heart, and buzzing happiness and passion throughout my veins I haven't felt in years.

Paris is life. The elegant and feminine architecture. The immaculately landscaped greenery, gilded with fairy lights and home to alfresco dining. I love the addictive people watching, so much more Zen than yoga.

My fingers crack as I stare at the couture dresses in the window of a boutique. My smile sends me floating, as memories of wanting a career in fashion design filter into my mind. My fingers dance, itching for a page to sketch the creations modelled in front of me. I breathe deeply, ready to soak up the inspiration and dreams living in this city.

Could I pursue it again?

Could I change from law to fashion school? Would I be any good at it? It's been so long since I've thought about it. All year I've focused on studying law... and nothing else.

So much wasted time.

Not only this year, but my last year of high school. When I should have been at parties, dancing and getting wasted. Instead, I got good grades and faded to the background.

Why did I give up on fashion? Sure, I couldn't dance post-accident, but I could still sketch. Nothing was wrong with my hands or eyesight. *Gah!* I'm so pissed at myself. Why did I allow myself to fall into this boring life? Because my good grades got Mum excited? Because Charli abandoned the plan and I wanted to fill the void? So our parents wouldn't be upset?

They still took their emotions out on her. I didn't save their relationship.

As if I did it for Charli.

It was fear. It was safe. It was a mistake.

I can't go back. I abandoned my plan so long ago. I can't undo this mistake. It'll mess up too much stuff for everyone else.

I hate myself. All these stupid decisions led me to such an unhappy place. My study could have given me joy. I could have been creating. I could have had bright days filled with hope. If I had decided what I wanted, and not tried to fill someone else's void.

Law is sucking the light out of me. Every day I live under the threat of a dark cloud, ready to unleash a dangerous storm. This is my life. No point trying to find a shred of happiness. May as well sink into the sad, black void, and stay numb to everything.

I meet Charli for lunch near our hotel, but the dark thoughts don't stop tumbling through my mind. Halfway through my salade niçoise, I drop my fork and apply pressure to my forehead.

"You ok?" Charli asks with concern.

"Massive headache," I hush. I scoot out my chair and stand. "I'm gonna go back to the room to rest."

"I'll walk you back," Charli offers.

I throw out a hand to stop her. "No, don't. Finish your lunch. Give me some time alone to get rid of this headache."

"Ok. No worries. I'll check on you later."

"Thanks."

Part of me is glad it was so easy to ditch Charli, but the fact it is easy to be alone weighs me down. I'm good at creating space around me and closing myself off, inside my head.

Worthless.

It's the only way to describe myself as I walk into our hotel room. I'm numb as I drag myself into the bathroom. It's clear to me I don't want to hurt myself. I want to find a meaningful life. Right now, I feel nothing.

With tears swarming my vision, I sift through my toiletries bag and pick up a razor blade. Ripping a blade through my flesh could be a wake-up call. Snap me out of this black hole and allow me to see again. To feel again.

It might help?

I slip Bryce's ring off my finger. His symbolic promise to always be with me, physically or not. I twist the gold band and watch the afternoon light dazzle the emerald stone. If I break the promise to stand by him, should I keep this ring off my finger?

Falling into my thoughts, the ring slips out of my grip. I lose sight of it but hear it clink against the tiles. I twist and scan the floor.

Shit!

Before my eyes, it vanishes in the floor drain. I scramble toward the drain which centres the tiled floor. The word *no* rushing out fast and furious. Water pools beneath the drain and there's no sign of the ring.

It's gone?

No...

It's gone.

10

Charli

I walk into our hotel room and place my key on a side table.

"Brit?" I call out.

I feel bad for spending the day without her, but I wanted her to enjoy her time here. I didn't want it to be like Bali, where I was pushing my agenda onto her. Paris is her happy place. Hopefully, the time alone helped her recharge.

I'm confused when I don't see her in bed, I thought she would be napping.

"Brit?" I call out again.

I stop by the bathroom door. I knock and the door creaks open, unhinging from the latch.

My eyes widen and my stomach leaps to my throat.

"BRITTANY."

I skid across the tile floor and reach Brittany, who slumps over in a t-shirt and underwear. Blood covers her left thigh and smears the tiles. Tears fill my eyes as I apply pressure to her bloody thigh.

"Brittany, what happened? Are you woozy? Can you talk to me?"

She lifts her chin and meets my eyes. Her eyes are grey with sadness and my heart splinters into a thousand pieces.

"Brittany?" I move a hand to her shoulder. "Can you stand? Do you need to go to a hospital?"

She shakes her head and with a croaky voice, says, "No. I don't need a hospital."

"Are you sure?"

She wipes a hand over her thigh. "It bled, but looks worse than it is. It's only two small cuts. They aren't deep."

A tear rolls down my face. "You cut yourself again?"

She shrugs, looking at her reddened thigh. "Felix said it was a good spot, and I was curious."

A gasp shoots out of me. "He wasn't suggesting you try it."

"It's not like it matters," she whispers, running a hand along her surgery scars. "The new scars will blend in with the rest."

My insides scramble.

A sigh sizzles out of her. "I wanted the pain gone."

I slump next to her. "Is being here no good?"

Brittany rests her head against the bathroom wall, her hair falling over her face, and a hint of a smile curling her lips. "Being here is wonderful. So wonderful it makes me hate my life. I hate everything I've been doing. I hate that I've been this fake piece of shit, existing for the sake of someone else." She grabs onto my wrist and whispers, "Why haven't I been living?"

"You have..."

She lifts her head and stares at the ceiling. "I wanna stay here. I wanna be French and pretend Sanford and everyone back home doesn't exist."

"You can go on an exchange program," I suggest.

Brittany scoffs. "No more school."

I nod. "Ok. No more school." I watch her wounds and there's a small amount of blood seeping out one cut, but most of the bleeding seems to have stopped. "Will you let me clean this up?"

She shrugs again.

"Maybe you should get in the shower to get rid of the blood?"

"Mhmm."

"I should get stuff from the pharmacy to ensure it's not infected. What did you cut it with? Was it rusty?"

She lifts her arm and a tiny blood-drenched piece of metal sits cupped in her palm.

I squint at it. "What is that?"

"A piece of a razor blade. I pulled it out of a razor that was new from its packet. It's clean."

"*Geez*, Brit. You're getting creative."

She blows out a breath. "I'm sick of everything."

I rub her arm. "What would you prefer? Bath or shower?"

She shakes her head. "I don't want to stand."

I help her over to the bathtub and out of her clothes. Bloodstained clothes to be incinerated. I let the water run and press a hand into the centre of Brittany's back to help her sit upright.

I don't trust her in the water alone. Once she's lowered into the bath, I sit on the edge with my feet in. She's dozy, so I cradle the back of her head, as I use my other to run a cloth down her body. I clench my core as I try to scrub her thigh and keep Brittany's head above water.

Maybe this was the worse choice, but what else could I have done? This was an absolutely shocking situation to walk into. I thought she was happy here. I thought the cutting was a one-time deal. I never would have guessed she'd cut herself, alone, on the tiles, in Paris. The city she's been in love with since we were ten-years-old. The place she's always dreamed of visiting. But her past crept up and stole her happiness. Her past is a relentless monster that won't let her be free, to start a life with thrilling new opportunities.

The water turns a murky brownish-red, and I pull the plug. As the water drains, I pull my arm out from under Brittany and I shake it, feeling like I've lifted a weight for an hour. It was the intense pressure of not wanting anything else to harm her. For wanting nothing *I do* to harm her.

She's groggy as I lift her out of the bathtub. The mass of running thoughts must have gotten to her. I wrap a bathrobe around her and we make our way slowly across the slippery and still bloody tiles. Once I get her to bed, I can clean up this room. As we make it across the carpet to her bed, I notice blood oozing below her robe.

"Shit, is it bleeding again?"

She nods. "Kinda stings."

"Shit. Ok, let's get you to bed and then I'll put some pressure on it. It should stop." I hope.

Brittany crawls on to the bed. She flops on her back and I push both palms onto her thigh. When I remove my hand, trickles of blood bubble from the cuts. I stretch beside the bed to my suitcase and snag a t-shirt. I wrap the cotton shirt around her thigh, hoping it'll soak up any more blood. Hopefully we won't soak every area of the hotel in Brittany's blood.

I leave her side and return to the bathroom. I soak my reddened hands under running water and gaze at the bloody footprints on the tiles. Do I just wipe this up with towels and throw them out before the hotel staff see? Or is this the kinda thing hotel staff are paid to clean up?

I swallow quickly and breathe in an ounce of bravery. *Just act quickly, Charli.* I gotta clean this up, get bandages and alcohol wipes, and then sit by Brittany's side until she stops feeling woozy.

I edge backward to the bathroom doorway. Shit. I hope she's ok over there and isn't passed out.

I run a couple of towels across the tiles for one quick, and almost useless, attempt at cleaning and then rush to Brittany's side to ensure she's breathing.

"You ok?" she asks, eyes wide open.

"*Phew.*" I clutch my racing heart.

"What's wrong?"

"Just my anxiety playing tricks on my mind. I'm going to clean the bathroom." I clutch her hand. "Stay right here."

She smiles. "Not going anywhere."

What a mess. Let's not put housekeeper on the list of potential career paths. Wanting to clean in a hurry, I used the bath nozzle to spray water over the tiles. Every towel is a sopping pink mess. I had to practically sandbag the bathroom doorway. Water was ready to seep into the carpet of the main room.

I used the towels to push water to the drainage. When the red ripples in the water drained away, I called it a day. Throughout all this, I had an overwhelming need for help. I do not know what I'm doing, and I'm scared I can't help Brittany in the way she needs. I mean, look at this. She's on a trip with me and she cut herself again. Am I really any help?

I just wish I had the skills to deal with this appropriately. To know how to clean up properly. To be able to help Brittany correctly with her wounds. To know what to say to her, or what to ask her. Or to know when to be silent and wait for her to talk, and know it's time to listen.

I wish I had paid attention to the nurses who took care of Brittany when she was in hospital after her surgeries. Instead, I was a selfish zombie. Volunteering helps me feel better without resorting to drugs. Like getting my hands dirty will help me stay clean. I should have acted like that the first time Brittany got hurt. I should have acted selflessly like the nurses who helped her every day. Instead, when I saw Brittany in the hospital bed, I'd wanna pass out, throw up, or just get high.

It's really tough on my own, trying to figure out what to do and not royally screw up. Especially when I'm winging it, and doubly tricky when in a foreign country and twenty-four hours from home.

I dash to the front door and hook the *Do Not Disturb* on the door handle. I then make it over to Brittany.

"Do you need me to run to the pharmacy and get bandages?"

"I think it's stopped bleeding. I think it bled again because I was moving. They were only small cuts, really."

"Ok, I'm glad. Just tell me if you need anything."

She frowns. "Sorry to be such a bother."

I clutch her hand and stare into her twinkling eyes. "You're important to me, Brittany. I'll do anything for you."

"I shouldn't have done something so shocking. You shouldn't have to walk in on that."

"Look at this," I say, angling my arm so she sees the kanji tattooed above the inside of my elbow. "This tattoo is your name."

"Huh?"

"It says, Brittany. I wanted your name because you are *that* important to me."

"But... why Japanese?"

"I wanted something in Japanese, but something I'd never regret. Something I'd love for always, no matter what."

Her index finger runs along the tattoo. "So, you branded my name on to you?"

A whisper of a laugh seeps out of me. "I wouldn't exactly put it that way, but yes."

She smiles. "You love me."

I kiss her cheek. "I love you. You're my number one, no

matter what."

She nods. "Right back at ya." She taps her single bed. "C'mon. Get in here and cuddle me."

"No problem," I say, and slide onto the bed next to her.

#

Last night was rough. It was tough to get a restful hour of sleep. I was constantly waking up, frantic to check on Brittany.

Thankfully, she slept soundly. All the conflicting thoughts in her head must be exhausting. I don't blame her. It's a shitty place to be. It was where I was at during high school.

With the ten-hour difference between Paris and Sydney, I used my insomnia to text with Bryce. The loneliness was getting to me and I needed someone to talk to. I don't want to complain to Brittany about how hard this is for me. That's not fair. But I need someone to lean on. Bryce is the person who will care the most.

I tried to be vague, but the more helpless I felt, the easier it was to let it slip.

I told him she cut herself.

She's going to kill me.

Is it totally selfish to reach out to her boyfriend because *I* needed help to deal with it?

Fuck.

She's going to kill me.

Brittany gets out of bed and tells me she's having a shower.

An ugly cramp seizes my stomach. "Don't lock the door," I say, as she walks across the room.

She *tsks* and enters the bathroom. She doesn't close the door, leaving it open ajar.

It is a mild relief.

The water runs and I debate whether to stand at the doorway. Creepy or necessary? I can't be by her side all the time. The way she huffed at me when walking to the bathroom is enough to know she wants some space. The fact the door is open is a sign she'll call for help when she needs it.

I'll just stay in bed for a few minutes. I'll get up when the water turns off. If the water runs for too long, I'll get up. If it sounds like she's fallen or any other strange noises, I'll get up.

Right now, I'm choosing to trust her.

When the water stops and her footsteps sound on the tiled floor, I call out, "You ok in there?"

"Yes, just let me dry my hair and do my makeup," she calls back.

"Ok."

Wow, makeup. Good for you, Brit. Not that makeup is important, but she likes it. It means something to her. It's major that she's using it after the disaster of yesterday.

I hear a *ping* beside me and wriggle to pick up the phone. I'm so sleepy I drop my hand before I can clutch the phone. I can't be bothered looking at the message right away. I close my eyes and a heavy call for sleep pulls at me.

"What the hell?" Brittany's voice thunder beside me, yanking me from sleep.

My eyes jolt open. "Huh?"

She tosses my phone at my bed. "You've been texting Bryce?" she wails, accusingly.

I launch to sitting, my hands up in defence. "I didn't do it to hurt you, I just…"

"You did exactly what I didn't want!"

"I'm sorry. I only meant to text him once, to let him know you're ok."

She plonks on her bed, a rage reddening her made-up face. "What is that supposed to mean?"

"I just kept in him the loop," I say sheepishly, regretting every character typed to Bryce.

"How could you?" she yells. "I told you I didn't want him to know."

"He couldn't be left to think the worst."

"It's not your decision! I saw your text, Charli. You've told him the worst!"

I shrink lower. "I'm sorry. I didn't mean to hurt you."

"Why didn't you just tell me you were talking to him?" Brittany asks, exhausted as her shoulders slump.

"You were so adamant about not wanting to talk to him. Every time I brought him up, I was looking for an opening to tell you. You always shut the conversation down."

"That should have clued you in to stop texting him."

"I'm sorry. I was scared."

Her eyes widen. "Scared?"

"I'm worried about you, and I'm alone. I needed someone else's help in what to do."

"You're not alone, we are together."

"Brittany, you're going through something major. You've cut yourself because of how deeply unhappy you are. I'm trying my best."

Her body shrinks. "You regret coming here with me?"

I launch over to her bed and wrap her in a hug. "Absolutely not. I'm glad you asked me to travel with you. This has been a dream. Well... if you were feeling better, it'd be the ultimate. I will never complain about time with you."

"Maybe we should go home," she whispers, collapsing in my arms.

"We've got two more days here. Let's relax and not put pressure on the rest of the trip."

"He knows I cut myself." There's defeat in her voice.

"Did you see his reply? He didn't lash out or throw shade. He's on your side, not matter what." I hug Brittany tighter, and add, "I only meant to tell him where we were going. I mean, someone had to know, in case of emergency. He wasn't telling Mum or Dad, or anyone else."

"Can we trust that? I trusted you not to talk to my boyfriend and look how that went."

I let her go. "Sorry."

She sighs. "I'm not mad at you. I appreciate why you did it. I was just hoping to bypass all this with Bryce. But looks like I'm gonna have to explain things to him now."

"I can be there to help."

"No. I know I'll eventually tell him everything. I was just looking for more time. The trip gave me that time, at least."

"Let's enjoy the rest of the trip. We can go to the museums, and a champagne bar, try snails, and catch a cabaret show."

She collapses next to me with an almighty grin. "I am so down."

11

Brittany

Charli helped me unpack in my dorm room. The inside of my room is chilling, so I suggest we take a walk before Charli leaves for work.

"*Ohmigawd*," I say, tapping Charli's shoulder excitedly as we stroll into campus. "It's Reece."

Charli's smile is ginormous. "Reece!" she calls out, waving madly.

Reece's head pans his immediate area until he lands on us. He waves and walks towards us.

"How are you?" Charli says, enthusiastically bouncing in place.

"I'm good. How are you both?" he replies.

"Really good," Charli says, brimming with delight at seeing

her friend.

"How are classes?" I ask Reece.

He nods. "Good. Yours?"

I tilt my head to the side, deciding on the best answer. "Not so good."

"Oh," he replies, emotionless.

"Brit's thinking of changing majors," Charli covers.

"Or just dropping out," I admit.

"Wow," Reece hushes. "I hope I still get to see you around campus."

I don't mean to, but I laugh. "We barely see each other."

Reece shrinks. "Sorry. I met some friends in my classes and I hang out with them. I guess I assumed you did the same thing. You are Miss Popularity, after all."

I blow a raspberry. "Miss Popularity? *Ha!*"

Charli clutches my hand. "Brit hasn't found her place yet."

"I'm sorry," I say to Reece. "I don't mean to be rude. I'm actually super happy you found new friends."

"Me too," Charli is quick to add. "I'm so proud of you, Reece."

Reece shrugs, a shy smile tugging at his lips. "Kellie helped me."

"Really?" Charli and I say at once.

"I see her," Reece says. He pivots between Charli and me. "Do you ever see her?"

"I think about her all the time," Charli says encouragingly. She lifts her t-shirt and hooks a thumb to lower her jeans. "She's in my skin so I never forget her."

Her green and purple peace sign tattoo hugs her hip, and Kellie's name proudly curves around it.

"She taught me never to be fake," Charli says, releasing her clothing. "To be my authentic self." She looks at the tattoos along her arm and laughs.

"Kellie would love how you look," I say. "She'd love how badass it is."

Reece looks Charli up and down. "Kellie *does* love it. She loves you."

Charli smiles wholeheartedly at him. "I know. Thank you, Reece."

"Perhaps the three of us can grab a bite to eat?" I suggest. "The *Apricot Café* on campus has the best coffee and cakes."

"It'd be awesome to hang out with you two again," Reece says, eyes wandering the cement path.

"I'm in, for sure," Charli cheers.

"We saw Nick a few weeks ago," I tell Reece as we walk along the path to the café.

"Is he well?" Reece asks.

"He seems good." I glance at Charli and snort. "His boyfriend is a bit much, though."

"That's one way to put it," Charli says. "He's a good guy. Fun but very eccentric."

"Flamboyant," I add.

She smirks. "Very flamboyant."

"Nick loves him?" Reece asks.

Charli stutters at the question.

I look at the clouds as I think about it. "I don't know. To be honest, I wasn't in the headspace to pay attention. Charli, did you notice if they said 'I love you'?"

"Um. I think I might have heard it."

"That would mean he's happy, wouldn't it?" Reece asks, hopefulness rising in his voice.

"I guess so," I reply. "Although, there was that one argument."

"Are you happy, Reece?" Charli asks with a moment of concern.

He stares ahead. "Yes."

"Are you worried about Nick?" she presses. "Do you know something we don't?"

He shakes his head. "No. I haven't spoken to him in a while. Just making sure he's ok."

"Why don't you visit him?" I suggest. "We both can go with you."

Reece's face tightens. "Will he want to see me?"

"Of course, he'll want to see you," Charli answers. "You two were so close in high school. What's happened? Why did you two stop talking?"

"Nothing happened, really," Reece mutters. "He started going out more and I don't like that noisy, crowded stuff."

"Ah," Charli says, clicking on the issue. "I get it. You started travelling in different circles. That makes sense."

I sigh. "That's what happened with Bryce and me."

"What?" Reece asks with surprise.

"He likes to go to parties, but I never feel comfortable," I say with a frown. "We stopped hanging out together and it's made things really weird between us."

"But you liked going out with Nick," Charli says with hope. "Can't things change with you and Bryce? Don't you think you'll want to go to parties with him?"

I shrug and whisper, "Maybe."

"I thought you and Bryce were solid," Reece says.

"We broke up twice in high school," I say flatly. "It's not very solid."

"After everything you two did to patch things up," Charli says, "I can't believe you keep saying that."

"Is that why you talk to him behind my back?" It just flies out.

Charli's mouth hangs open. She halts in place. Reece looks back and forth between us.

I groan.

"I'm not mad at you," I grizzle. "I just want you to stop playing Team Bryce. Just side with me on everything. Please?"

"There shouldn't be any doubt I'll always side with you."

I smile and nod.

"What did I miss?" Reece asks slowly.

"Nothing," Charli and I say in unison.

I bite into my lip as I notice a distinct look in Charli's eye. "What?"

Her shoulders bunch high. "I was just wondering..." Her eyes dart between Reece and me.

"*Ugh.* Just say it."

"Why haven't you seen Bryce yet?" Charli blurts. "Just let him know you're back."

"He's been texting you, hasn't he?" I accuse.

"Because you don't answer him," she admits.

I stamp my foot. "Can't I just settle in?"

"I can go with you," Charli offers. She looks at Reece and smiles. "After we catch up with Reece. We can find Bryce together. If you want the support."

I'm so over this.

I back away with my hands up. "Forget it."

"What?" her voice is small.

"Sorry Reece," I say. "We'll catch up later. I'm going to see Bryce so Charli can stop talking about him."

"Wait," Charli says. "Don't go if you're angry."

"I'm not angry," I say as I storm off, leaving the pair in my dust.

I bang on Bryce's door. My blood pumps hard, and I'm too riled up to give in now.

"Bryce!" I call through the door as I continue to pound.

When there's no response, I check the time on my phone. I'm still getting back on schedule after the jetlag, so I'm unsure if he has a class now or not.

How can I forget? Paying attention to him is literally my only hobby.

"Brit?" his voice sounds in the hall.

I turn to him and shiver.

Why does he look so freaking good? His butterscotch hair has that effortlessly tousled look. His rosy lips appear full in the best way. His topaz eyes twinkle like their elated to be staring at me.

"Hi," I say, just audibly.

He rushes towards me and wraps me in a hug.

Neither of us say a word.

His hug is strong, and in a state of shock, I barely touch him. I'm back in his presence, and he's glad to see me. I'm still working out how I feel about this.

"Did you just get back?" he whispers, his face brushing against my hair.

"Pretty much."

Bryce lets me go and takes a step back. His head tilts as he looks at me, and he asks, "Are you ok? *Truly* ok?"

I bite into my lip and shrug. I don't know how to answer.

He gestures to his door. "D'you wanna come in?"

"Sure."

Bryce unlocks the door and I follow him inside. He keeps his head low as he walks to his desk, fiddling with the key and taking his time to place it on the desk and turn back to me.

I slide my back against a wall, arms tucked behind my back like a defensive move to not talk first.

"You were just gone one day," Bryce says, sadness drooping his face as he looks me up and down. "What happened? Why didn't you want to talk to me about it?"

"I just needed to get away."

He sits on the edge of his bed with a tired sigh. "I get it. But a text would have been nice. A heads up. I didn't know what to think."

Behind my back, I trace the healing wound on my wrist.

"What would you have done if I told you?"

The iciness of my tone must have shocked him, because a tear escapes his eye.

"I didn't know what to do," I offer. "I wasn't thinking clearly."

Bryce stands and moves close to me. "All I care about is that you're safe." His hands cup my hips. "You're here now, and I'm so glad."

His face edges closer to mine, and when he attempts to kiss me, I pull away.

"Don't."

"What did I do?" he asks, the hurt radiating on his face.

"I just don't want to kiss right now."

"No, I mean, to want me out of your life when you were hurting. Did I do something to make you so unhappy?"

Annoyance rolls my eyes. "My emotions don't have to be all about you."

"Brit, I know that. I just want to help you." He brushes a piece of hair off my face. "I love you and I've missed you."

"I love and miss you too." I sound like a total robot. What am I doing?

"Do you wanna talk about what happened while you were away?"

"Why? Don't you already know everything?"

He takes half a step back, his eyes narrowing with confusion.

I push off the wall. "Charli."

"Yeah, we texted, but it was *you* I wanted to talk to."

"You were talking with Charli behind my back," I snap, shoving him hard.

"Because you weren't talking to me," he replies, his tone calm as he regains his balance. "I'm so thankful your sister reached out."

I groan in frustration and plonk onto the edge of the bed.

"You are mad at me?" He kneels in front of me. "Tell me what I did wrong. Please? I want to fix it."

I huff and shuffle further up the bed so he's not in front of me.

"Brittany? Brittany, talk to me."

"Stop it."

"Stop what?"

"You should have let me have time alone. You shouldn't have made my sister give you intel on me."

"I didn't make her do anything," he says, standing. "She wanted to tell me and keep me in the loop. I just wish I was by you."

I huff and stamp a foot. "You're a broken record. I don't have to do anything."

He clutches my hand and there's desperation in his expression. "I want to take care of you."

My face droops. "You don't want to take care of this mess."

His fingers interlace with mine. "What?"

"This isn't what you want. You don't want to know about my stuff."

"Yes, I do. That's literally all I've been saying."

I shake off his hand, get off the bed, and walk to the other side of the room

"No, you're saying all the right things," I huff. "The things a good boyfriend is supposed to say." I lift my wrist. "When his twisted girlfriend does this."

"I want to help you." He gently takes my wrist. "I don't want this to happen to you again."

I reef my hand back. "It's not up to you."

"Are you saying I can't help?"

My heart rampages inside me. I turn away from him to help it slow down.

"How can you say I can't help?" his voice is fragile.

"Bryce, stop."

"You know I'm always here for you. That's why I got you that ring. Oh... you took it off?"

"I lost it." It cuts deep to say it aloud. "In Paris."

"Oh. I'm sorry."

I shrug it off.

"Why won't you talk to me?" His hands run down my arms and leave goosebumps. "What has happened to us? We shouldn't keep secrets from one another."

My hands slide over my face, and I listen to his breath behind me. I agree with him, but I'm still decisionless.

"I'm scared," he whispers.

At that, I lower my hands. I turn to him and shake my head. "I'm scared."

"Why didn't I know you were so upset? Depressed?" The questions are directed at himself, not me.

"You didn't want to know," I croak as a sob comes out mid-sentence.

Bryce takes a step back. "What do you mean I don't want to know?"

"You're happy being happy." I backtrack to the door. "You don't want my problems."

"How can you say that?" he asks, standing in place. "I love you. I can take on your problems. We do that for each other."

"You told me you want to forget everything that happened. That you want a fresh start here. To move on from depression."

"That doesn't mean I won't help with yours. I'm sorry I didn't see the signs. Maybe I was making myself blind to it. But it doesn't mean I love you any less. I'm here for you and I always will be."

I deadpan him as I sniff back tears. "Don't say things you don't mean."

"I mean it, Brittany." He taps at his heart. "I've never lied to you."

"No." I frown hard, my hand clutching the doorknob. "I'm the one ruining this relationship."

"Brittany," he says breathlessly, taking both my hands. "What is happening? Just talk to me. I want to know everything. Everything that is wrong. Let me help you."

I fling his arms off and press against the door. "Just stop! Stop pressuring me."

"Pressuring you? I want to know what's going on. I'm in this relationship too."

"*Just stop,*" I scream, pulling at my hair, my heart racing and ricocheting off my ribs. "*Just stop. I can't do this anymore.*"

My volume sends him backward. I reef the door open.

"What are you saying?" he stammers, fear dripping off his words. "What are you going to do?"

I race into the hall and run without answering him.

"Brittany, Stop! Come back!"

I don't stop. My heart pounds in my throat and pain shoots into my ears and down my back. My eyes prick with hot tears. I race down the stairs with shallow breathes until I'm out of the dorm.

My chest strains from lack of breath, and I almost double-over on the lawn. But I can't stay here. I can't be here. I can't do this.

I've got to get out.

I've got to get out now.

12

Charli

"Wow. What you're studying sounds fascinating," I say, looking over Reece's textbook as we sit at the campus café. "I can't believe you get into such deep topics."

"It is fun," Reece says in a flat tone.

I smirk. So Reece.

"I'm glad you find it fun," I say. "You seem happy here."

He nods. "It is good."

"Reece?" a female voice says from behind us. Over my shoulder, a pretty brunette girl with fair skin and a smattering of freckles waves at us. "Hey."

I wave back as Reece says, "Hi Kendal."

"Hi," Kendal says, stopping by us. She looks at me, back at Reece, and her jaw flexes as her eyes land on me. "Hi, I'm

Kendal."

I smile and reply. "I'm Charli. Can't wait for Reece to do the introductions, huh." I look at Reece, who seems to not understand the awkwardness occurring.

Kendal moves by Reece's side, turning away from me. "How are you today, Reece?"

"I'm well," he replies.

"That's good. Cole, Lane, and I are studying in the library tonight at six pm. Do you want to join us?"

Reece nods and says, "Sure. That will be good."

Kendal eyes me and then turns back to Reece. She touches Reece's shoulder firmly and says, "Ok, see you then." She eyes me again. "Hope you have a good day."

"You too," I reply.

"Bye," Kendal says, backing away slowly.

Reece says goodbye as Kendal moves further towards a courtyard.

"So, Kendal, huh?" I begin. "What's going on there?"

"Whaddaya mean?"

"She seems very smitten with you."

"She's my friend."

"She seems to want more than friendship."

Reece nudges me. "Shuddup. Don't start stories."

"Well, Kendal was looking at me with daggers. She's definitely feeling something special toward you."

"Speaking of stories," Reece changes the subject, "are you still writing?"

"I dabble." I trace the quill tattooed on my forearm. "It's still a super important part of my life. I write online under an alias."

"Ever consider coming to university to pursue it further?"

"Sometimes I do. But I never finished high school, so I have major red tape to get through."

"I can help you with it," Reece offers. "It'd be nice to see you more often."

"Aw, you too, Bud." I attempt to ask him more about uni life, but my phone rings.

Incoming Call - Bryce.

"Hello?" I answer.

Bryce is breathless with anxiety. "Is Brittany with you?"

"No, what's happened? You sound worried."

"She ran out of here and I don't know what she's going to do. She didn't sound like herself. I'm worried about her. She doesn't want me around her, but she needs help. Can you help? I don't know where she is. Can you help me find her? I don't... I don't..."

"*Whoah*, Bryce, take a breath," I interrupt his rapid and manic sentences. I stand and step a few feet away from Reece. "Take a seat and just breathe. I need you collected if you're going to help Brittany. Now, what happened? What did she say?"

"I was asking her to explain what was happening because I wanted to help her. She just kept saying she couldn't do this and she couldn't be here. Does that mean she'll...?"

I rub the pain out of my chest. "Bryce, don't go there. It won't be helpful right now. We just have to find her. I'm sure it was the confrontation that was too much for her. She's having trouble admitting her struggles to you. I don't know why, but we need to accept that you're a sore spot right now. I'm sorry, I know it's hard to take."

He sighs. "It's fine. I just want to know she's safe."

"Where are you right now?"

"I'm near her dorm room. We were in my room when she left."

"Ok, stay there in case she comes back to reconcile things. I'll have a look around campus for her and keep you posted."

"Don't tell her we talked. She doesn't like that we've been messaging."

"Keeping it a secret won't help. I'll call you when I'm with her. She has to know we're both looking out for her. Please try to stay calm. I'll find her. I promise."

I slide my phone into my pocket and walk back to Reece.

"What was that about?" Reece asks.

"I'm sorry, I've got to go."

"Is it Brittany? Is she ok?"

"I think she will be. I just need to find her. Will you text me if you see her?"

"Sure thing. Text me later to let me know you two are ok."

I smile. "Will do."

My feet ache as I pound the pavement. I rack my brain, deciding where Brittany would go to think on her issues. As I run through campus, my eyes peeled for Brittany, I'm distracted by a sign. *Film Lab.* My pace slows and my hand rubs against the slow beat of my heart.

The building draws me in. My fingers creep around my neck

and intertwine below my head. The chance of seeing him is so miniscule, but something is telling me to look. Like, maybe, just maybe, he'll be here.

I hug my waist, peering down a pathway, but then I back away, accepting that it is crazy to think he'd be there. I stop as a group of students pass me by. I wait to follow behind them and then the air is snatched from my lungs.

He slings a backpack over one shoulder. He has the same dishevelled handsomeness he had in high school, but he's lost his gorgeous curly locks. His brunette hair is now cropped short.

But it's him.

It's Travis.

A deliciously ecstatic smile takes over my face. I tug on the belt loops of my jeans and rock on the balls of my feet, waiting for him to look my way.

He glances at me and then turns away.

I hold a breath.

He looks up and then back at me. His lower lip drops. He stops mid-step. He turns toward me.

I breathe again.

He mouths, 'hi.'

I raise a hand to wave.

He moves towards me as I move towards him. Within moments, I leap forward and I'm in his arms. My hands are fast to his face. I cup his chin and I plant my lips on his. His hand plays in my hair as the other presses into my back.

His kiss is just as I remember. Warm, perfect pressure with a bit of suction. I run my hands down to his shoulders and onto his chest.

He lets out a breathy laugh as our lips part. "Took me a second to realise it was you."

I note my tattooed arm. "I look different, huh?"

He brushes back part of my brunette hair. "Just a little."

Travis lowers me to the ground. I smile and touch the cropped sides of his hair as I say, "And what about you. What did you do to your hair?"

He laughs. "What do you mean?"

"All your curls are gone."

He nods at me. "So are yours."

I clap my hands over my mouth and laugh.

"What are you doing here?" he asks, rubbing my shoulders.

"I'm here with..." I pinch the bridge of my nose and wince. "Ah, I have to find Brittany. Sorry, I gotta go, but can we meet up later?"

He releases me and takes a step back. "Sure, I have a class to get to, anyway. Are you free tonight? There's this bar on campus called *The Pit*. D'you know it? Meet me at seven?"

I nod. "I'll be there." I touch his cheek and smile. "It's so good to see you."

Travis takes my hand and squeezes it. "You too."

In a hurry, I race along the cement path with no idea where I'm going. One thought in my head. I'm choosing to make Brittany a priority.

My phone buzzes in my pocket. While running, I read the message.

I text him thanks and pull up the campus map to find the location.

"Brittany!" I call out as my heart thunders in my chest. *"Brittany!"*

She sits on a rock overlooking the school below. I'm breathless as I reach her.

"Oh, Brit, I was so worried." I wrap my arms around her and kiss her forehead. I drop to sit beside her and race to catch my breath. "Are you ok?"

She's limp beside me. Her face is solemn, her skin is dull, and there is no twinkle in her eyes.

"Brit?"

"I'm ok," she whispers.

"Bryce called me."

She groans. "Of course he did."

"He's worried," I say, pulling out my phone. "Let me call him."

She places a hand over my phone. "Don't."

"I promised him I would."

"So, what he says matters more than what I want?"

"Brit, don't be like that. He's hurt too."

She huffs and removes her hand. "Fine, whatever. Call him, but I'm not talking to him."

"That's fine," I say, clicking *call* on Bryce's contact page. He answers immediately. "Hello?"

"She's ok," I say quickly. "She's with me and she's fine."

"Oh, thank goodness. Can I talk to her?"

"Not right now."

"I just want to apologise. Please tell her. Tell her I want to say sorry."

I lower the phone. "Brit?"

"I'm not speaking to him," she's quick to say.

"He wants to apologise."

She turns away from me.

I gulp and lift the phone to my ear. "Not right now, Bryce. She needs a little time. We'll call you later."

"Take care of her, Charli."

"I will. Take care of yourself too."

I hang up and look back at Brit. "What happened?"

She tenses. "Didn't your buddy Bryce tell you everything?"

"Don't be like this. Don't close me out. He called me because he's worried about you. He loves you, Brit."

"I know!" she snaps. A flood of tears surge from her eyes and she hunches over, covering her face and shuddering in sobs.

"Oh, Brit," I hush, hugging her close and rubbing her back. "Brit, it's ok. Just take your time. Take all the time you need."

"It's just hard," she sobs against my chest.

"I know," I hush, brushing back her hair. "I know it is."

She sits up and wipes her eyes. "I don't want to be mad at him."

"It's ok. Are you mad at him? Did he do something you haven't told me about?"

Her jaw clenches and she breathes tightly, like she's holding something back.

"Brit?"

"I think I resent him."

"Really?"

"Yeah. He's doing really well... and I'm jealous."

I bite inside my cheek, searching for something reassuring to say.

"I think I'm sick of looking at him," she says, her face tense as she ponders the statement.

I hold my breath, staring at her, and suddenly, she breaks into laughter. She pats her puffy eyes and presses her hands into her reddened cheeks. All signs of her crying, now morphing into laughter.

"You ok?" I ask, hesitant.

She reclines back. "It's just a relief to say it out loud."

I lean in and kiss her forehead. "Oh, I'm so glad you feel better."

"Does it make it worse that I don't want to talk to him? I just feel done. I don't want to go through it again."

"Ask yourself how you would feel if the roles were reversed. What did you do regarding his mum and the eating disorder? You took a step back, but you were around when he needed you. Can't you set those boundaries again? In reverse?"

She takes a breath out. "Yeah, I guess. I just want to talk to you about this stuff. No one else."

I smile, rubbing my warming heart. "Honestly, Brit, that's the best thing I've ever heard in my entire life. But Bryce loves you, and he's such a great guy. I love him like a brother, and it hurts me to see you be so cold to him."

Brittany sits up straight and looks down at the buildings below. "I know. I have to be kinder to him. Somehow let him in."

I rest an arm across her shoulders. "I'm proud of you, Sis."

She grins at me. "Thanks, Sissy."

"You want to hear about the strangest, weirdest thing that just happened?"

She tilts her head. "Other than this?"

I blurt it out, "I just saw Travis."

She gasps, "*Get out.*"

"I kissed him before saying hello."

She whacks my arm. "You kissed him? What do you mean you kissed him?"

Nervous laughter seeps out of me. "I don't know. It was electric. It was like I couldn't help it. It was magnetic. It was animalistic. It was destiny."

She puffs a laugh. "Shuddup. It was slutty."

I whack her arm. "Shuddup. Don't call me a slut."

"You kissed him straight up."

"I'm just trying to share something with you. Like, distract you."

"Well, go on, share. What happened?"

"It was on the way here."

She raises an eyebrow. "You made out with him instead of coming directly here?"

"I'm telling you, it was like something overtook my body. It was like I *had* to do it."

"You're ridiculous."

I rest a head on her shoulder. "It was wonderful."

"Travis Watkins, we're talking about?"

I laugh. "Yes, what other Travis is there?"

"You're swooning over Travis Watkins? What is wrong with you?"

I groan and lift my head. "Grade ten was a long time ago."

Brittany looks at me with disappointment.

I frown. "Stop with that look."

She double-downs on the look.

I smirk. "You're the worst."

"So, you just kissed him?" she asks. "I don't understand how you can just do that. Have you seen him since high school?"

I shake my head slowly, biting my lip as I think about all the visuals I've created in my head over the last year.

Her eyes narrow. "Why are you looking like you have?"

"I've just thought about him a lot. I've kinda really been wanting to run into him... and today was the day."

"*Ohmigawd*, you want him back?"

"I'm meeting up with him tonight," I say, grinning. "We will see how it goes."

"*Ugh*, the worst. Can't you see how much of a bad idea this is?"

"Don't be like that." I raise my arm and turn it in and out to show off the tattoos. "We've all changed since high school."

Brittany lifts her scarred wrist. "Yes, we have."

My smile fades and I take Brittany's wrist. I touch the raised scar and frown at her. "When are you going to see Bryce again?"

She sighs and rests her head on my shoulder. "When do you think I should?"

"We can go to see him together. Get it over with now."

"Mmm, not now."

I place my hand over the shape of my phone in my pocket. "I think he might still be at your room. I had told him to wait for you."

Brittany raises her head, gasping, "WHAT?"

"I thought you might go back there while I was looking for you."

"*Geez*, get him out of there right now."

I pull out my phone and open the 'Bryce' text chain. My fingers tremor before I type.

Brittany reefs the phone from me. "I'll do it." She furiously types and then shoves the phone back at me. "There."

I look down at the phone screen.

(Me) Get out of her room now.

"Brittany," I scold.

"What?"

"I don't talk to him like that."

Her eyes slit at me. "What? Not precious enough? Since when are you two besties, anyway?"

I groan and roll my eyes, and I slide the phone into my pocket. I'll text him later to smooth things over.

"I dunno," I begin. "I want things to work out between you two. I like you two together. But maybe I'm changing my mind now. Maybe you two are better off without each other."

Brittany chews her lower lip, folds her arms across her chest and looks over at the buildings below.

I take a slow breath out as the noise around us fills our silence. I really don't have a clue what to say to her to make any of this ok. Maybe I was a jerk to look for Travis.

But it's Travis.

He was right there.

How could I not?

When I walk into *The Pit,* my eyes take a moment to adjust to the dank lighting. Conversations yell over the live band in the crowded seating area.

My boots have a tall heel, yet I tiptoe for a better view. I crane my neck, but maybe I've gotten here before him. As I step around a few tables, I spy him. He stands by a table, tapping a beer glass.

Excitement bubbles inside me as his gaze lifts. Light dances in his dark eyes as he rounds the table. I move quickly toward him and throw my arms up and wide. I run my hand around the back of his neck and lean in close to his lips.

He stops me.

"Wait," he whispers, his hand pressing down on my shoulder.

"What?"

"Can we sit?" he asks, nodding to a table.

"Yeah, ok."

As we each take a bar stool at the high cocktail table, he says, "Don't get me wrong, it is great to see you again."

I squint at him. "Ok?"

He sighs and rubs his brow. "I have a girlfriend."

"Oh." I slide down the seat slightly.

He takes my hand. "I just got so caught up in seeing you. It was like nothing had changed. I felt the exact same way about you."

I rub my lips together and take a breath. "So, it's serious?"

"We've been together for six months."

I nod and swallow uncomfortably. I note how nice his thumb feels, rubbing gentle circles against my hand.

"I'm sorry I didn't think to ask," I say.

He lets out an uneasy laugh and releases my hand. "We didn't have time for greetings before we kissed."

"Should I not have kissed you?"

"I kissed you back." He looks around the room and then back at me. "I take it you're not with anyone?"

I shake my head. "I don't really do relationships."

"Oh?"

I push for a smile. "Because I've only wanted you."

Travis chokes on air. "Wh-what?"

I slide a hand over my mouth and muffle my bashful laugh.

He leans in close, his dark, almond eyes mesmerising me. "What does that mean?"

I shrug and twirl a piece of hair around a finger. "I just think about you. A lot."

"Why?" He's genuinely dumbfounded.

"Because I miss you."

"You've never said anything."

"I didn't think I could."

"I thought I was the one not allowed to contact you."

He touches my hand again. This time his fingers gently stroke my fingers. It sends tingles up my arm and down my body. Damn, boy.

I clear my throat. "I need a drink."

He nods and checks his empty glass. "Me too. What can I get you?"

"Vodka tonic."

He pats my shoulder and smiles. "Keep our table safe and I'll be right back."

When he leaves for the bar, I breathe out a very, very, long breath. Wow. I'm at a bar with Travis. *Travis.* We're together, in the same place. Again. Finally. Wow. Can I actually do this?

He comes back with our drinks, and I take two big mouthfuls before we pick up where we left off.

After a few drinks, we're giggly. His smile is so damn cute. I lean into him a few times, keeping my head down and away in that flirty way. His hand runs down my back.

He tells me about changing majors from business, like his dad wanted, to studying film production like he'd dreamt about. Tingles sliver through my body when he explains I helped him take the leap. In the five minutes we chatted at Kellie's memorial, what I said about following his passions changed the course of his life. I giggle, remembering I still have the jacket he lent me that night in my closet.

On another lean in, I get close to his neck. Man, he smells so good. Mint and vanilla, just as I remember. My hand lifts, wanting to plant on his chest, but I pull back. My head tilts, and my lips desperately want contact with his neck.

I'm sure he feels my breath on his neck as he plays with my hair. A guy doesn't play with a girl's hair if he's not interested. I smile and lean in until I'm met with flesh. A breathy moan leaves his lips like he's wanted to ask me to do that all evening.

The heel of his palm nudges my shoulder, but not enough to say he hates this.

"Charli," he whispers.

I remove my lips and search his face. "Yes?"

His lips curl as he jiggles in a silent laugh.

I lift my eyebrows and smirk. "Yes?"

"You're being bad," he whispers, laughing.

I bite my lip and smile. "Me? Never."

He curls a finger and runs it down my cheek.

I tilt my head, smiling.

"Stop it," he whispers.

"Stop what?"

He laughs and shakes his head. "Fuck it." He runs his hand into my hair and pushes his lips onto mine.

I hold on to him like a life-preserver. I kiss him with a burning passion, for all the nights I imagined this moment and never ever thought it would happen.

"You want to get out of here?" he whispers and then kisses the spot below my earlobe.

I hold on to the collar of his shirt with a mighty grip and

kiss him hard. "Yes, please."

We leap off our bar stools and round the tables with our hands clasped tightly together. A jittery giggle spills out of me, and I lean into him to keep my balance on my high heels.

When we step outside the bar, Travis gives me an apprehensive yet cheeky smile. His chest puffs and then quickly deflates.

"You're sure?" I ask, fingers crossed behind my back.

He pulls me close and kisses me feverishly.

I giggle as we pull apart. "Ok, you're sure."

"My dorm room is just a few blocks this way," he says, swinging my arm and nudging his head backwards. "Is that ok?"

I nod my head like it might pop up. "I'd love to see where you live."

We speak little on the walk, although our hands do a lot of the talking. We sling our arms along each other's lower backs, and then I take a bold step of cupping his bum. It must have been a good move because he then does the same to me.

He fumbles with his keys at his door because I'm pawing at him and kissing along his jawline.

He laughs as he has trouble fitting his key into the lock. "Stop it. I can't do it."

"*Shoosh.* That's the last thing a girl wants to hear."

Laughter tumbles out of him as he finally unlocks the door. We are both in fits of giggles as we enter his room. I love looking at the back of his closed door and push him against it. I recall all the wonderful memories of being alone with him and attack his lips like I'm making up for lost time.

For all the times I've wanted him.

For all the times I was mad about how things ended.

For every time I was angry at other people for turning him into a monster I didn't know. A monster they wanted. A monster who would forget who I was and what we meant to each other.

I search his eyes and tease his bottom lip. He hasn't forgotten me. He smiles. His hands run the length of my midsection. He still wants me.

I'm going to have him.

We kiss as we move towards the bed, somehow spinning in circles. Mimicking his grin, I pull off his shirt and throw it to the ground. His hands play at the waistband of my skinny jeans, he flicks the buckle, but then his hands jerk away.

"What?" I ask breathily, gripping his waist and pulling him towards me.

"Are you really ok with this?" he asks.

"Yes. I'm here, aren't I?" I brush a hand through his cropped hair.

"I don't want to make you uncomfortable or take advantage of you."

"Darling, you couldn't." My hand runs down his chest, abdomen, and then cups the nice bulge in his pants. "If anything, I'm taking advantage of you."

His smile widens, and in one swift move, he lifts me up and my legs wrap around his waist. I run my hands along his jaw and kiss him hard.

"I want you so bad, Travis Watkins."

"I've never stopped wanting you."

He lays me on the bed, and his kisses are soft and sweet. He touches my body gently and I realise I still have all my clothes on and he still has his damn pants on.

This I have to change. I move a hand between his legs and a breathy moan seeps out of him. I unbutton the small clasps on the front of my lace top and reveal my sheer black bra. His jaw flexes and his lips wet.

Just grab my boobs already.

I unzip his fly and notice how much work I'm doing. I turn us until he lies on his back and I'm on top. I understand why he's standoffish, so I need to take total control.

I shimmy his pants down as I sit on his lap. As my lace top lands on the floor, his fingers creep up my torso. I catch them and slide them over my bra.

Travis smiles and lets out an easy breath. His body relaxes in a way he hasn't all night. He cups my breasts and I unhook the clasps at the back. As the straps fall down my shoulders, he pulls himself up to sitting.

His hands move around to my back, and he holds my body close to his. Our chests press together in a moment so pure I want it sealed into my memory. My face rests against his shoulder, as our bodies rise and fall in sync.

I kiss his cheek, and he strokes my hair.

"You're so beautiful," Travis whispers.

His eyes run down my body and his hand brushes against the roses on my ribs. "You look so different, but also, exactly the same." He squeezes my thigh right below the phoenix tattoo. "Beautiful."

"You're as handsome as I remember you."

I push him back against the bed and lay on top of him. We kiss like high school kids. I can't get enough of his body against mine. I could stay like this forever. I literally need nothing more in life. This feeling is more than incredible.

I love him.

My breathing stops and I pull my lips away from his. My forehead scrunches.

I love him? We said those three little words to each other countless times. I still feel it?

Yes. How could I not? Of course, I still love him.

Our arms wrap each other up, and my thighs creep around him. I am ready for more. And it feels like he is ready for more. I smile at him, biting my lip, and he smiles back at me. He unravels his arms from behind my back and I sit up on his lap. I am ready to be with him. I am ready to take him in. I am ready to be one with this boy and really feel his love in an ultimate way.

We lay together as the sunrise nears, wrapped in each other's arms. Loose yet tight. Travis kisses my forehead and I could melt into him.

He frowns. "I'm sorry."

I lift my head so I can see his face. "Sorry?"

Sadness wrinkles his forehead. "I'm dating someone else."

"Oh." I rub his arm. "It's ok."

"It's not. I shouldn't have done this. I should have ended it with her before starting up with you."

I gently touch his face. "But we both wanted this."

"It wasn't respectful though."

I pull him close. "I don't care that you're dating someone else. You haven't disrespected me."

"I'm not interested in being the guy who is horrible to his girlfriend. I don't want to be known as that guy."

I let him go. "Oh, you regret being with me tonight?"

He pulls me in. "No. No, of course not."

"You feel bad for her?"

He nods, lips down-turned.

"You love her?"

He shakes his head. "No."

I exhale with the hint of a smile. "Ok."

His hands run down my back, and he says, "I'm so grateful to be with you. I love you."

My heart beats loudly in my chest. "You love me?"

He nods and kisses my lips. "I love you."

It's magnificent to hear those three words come from his lips again.

Smiling, I gaze deeply into his eyes, and say, "I love you too."

In the later hours of the morning, we wake in an unbreakable embrace.

"How'd you sleep?" he asks, blinking his eyes open.

"Glad you were holding onto me, or I might have rolled out of this single bed."

He kisses my cheek. "I won't let anything harmful happen to you."

I snuggle into his warmth, and reply, "I'll protect you. You got a girlfriend, huh? How are you planning to deal with that one?"

"As quickly as possible," he says with a sigh.

"Breakups are too hard. That's why I never make a serious commitment. I can't stand the goodbyes."

"You haven't had many relationships?"

"I've had relationships, just not anything I would call boyfriend or girlfriend material."

"Oh, wow. So, you date both guys and girls?"

"Yeah. Is that ok?"

"It's ok with me. I just didn't know."

"It's no big deal."

"You've been ok? With the lack of commitment?"

"I think I've been waiting for you. Something told me yesterday I would find you. Who knew my dream would come true?"

He laughs, his cheeks growing pink. "Are you calling me your dream?"

I giggle. "Yeah."

He lifts himself up. "I need to break up with her. I need only you in my life."

I pull him down beside me. "Not now. You stay and cuddle with me. You can deal with that ugly business later. Let's just soak up all this goodness as long as we can. Until the sickly sweetness makes us puke."

"You have such a way with words, my poet." He laughs and nestles beside me. "I'm never letting you go again. Never, ever. It's you and me forever, ok?"

I giggle and wrap myself around him. "Forever and ever."

He kisses my nose. "For always."

13

It's definite.

I'm dropping out.

Sitting in my tutorial, looking around at my peers, I don't belong here. I want more. I want fun. I want passion.

But I'm shit-scared.

How do I tell Mum and Dad? Will they cut me out like they did Charli? It's not the money that worries me, it's not being able to call whenever I need help.

Charli can call home whenever she wants. I honestly think she doesn't want to. But there's huge awkwardness between her and our parents. I don't want that. I still want to feel safe when I go home. To either home.

I wish I could hash this out with someone else. Form a game

plan to get out of this whole uni thing. I could talk to Nick about this, but what if it got back to Dad? Nick respects Dad so much, and I don't want to ruin what they have by making Nick keep secrets.

I scroll through my phone contacts and land on Madi. Madi can be a great listener, and she's tough as nails. But she's best friends with Nick and a gossip. She'd spill or hint at things, and that just puts me back in the same position.

I need someone who has no ties to Sanford. *Gah!* Why didn't I make any new friends during classes?

My aimless scrolling lands on Will Maclean. I haven't talked to Will in forever, but that goes for everyone. He left Sanford during high school. I bet he wouldn't say anything. He had such vicious rumours spread about him. But he and Bryce aren't exactly on great terms. Bryce never truly forgave Will.

If I can't talk to my boyfriend about all this, imagine how he'd feel if I talked to Will? I was so mad when he spoke to Charli behind my back. Uh, I just couldn't do it.

Charli is the only person I can trust. The only person who gets me. Or the only person I want to understand me. Bryce and I have been through so much. He knows me so well, but I don't want his pity. I don't want him to be with me out of guilt. I don't want him to pretend for my sake.

I'd hate to have confirmation he does any of those things. I just want to run from him.

My finger drags over the raised scar across my wrist. The familiar nagging inside dares me to do it again. I flip my wrist over and plant the scar against my desk.

Never again.

How would Mum react? I distinctly remember the pride on her face the first time I told her I was considering studying law. Will I get the opposite now? Anger? Hurt? Apathy?

She always said I was smart, and before grade twelve, I showed no interest in law. It's not like it was a lifetime ambition. It was a last-minute switch after the obliteration of a potential dance career. Not that dance was my end game. It was a hobby.

What did I used to dream about? I remember loving sewing and textiles classes. I loved design and creating. I was good at maths and social sciences, but the classes I really felt a passion for were textiles and design.

A smile tingles at my lips, and I slide my chin into my palm. I did have a dream of fashion design. Having my own label. Seeing my creations on a runway. London, Paris, Milan. That's why being in Paris hurt. I hate that I have such a horrible memory of my favourite city on Earth. Paris reminded me of buried memories. The pain forgetting has caused. It throbbed in my gut, and in my heart.

I shouldn't forget that hurt. I should use it to move forward. For once, move in a positive direction. What am I waiting for?

Can I just talk to Mum? Can she text Dad my new plan? *Ohmigawd*, no way am I talking to them at the same time. Imagine the two of them ganging up on me. *Ugh*. No, thank you. Tara would have to be there for sure.

Wow.

Just thinking about Tara gives me relief. She's such a cheerleader. I really don't think any of us kids can do any wrong in her eyes. She's always there, ready to give support.

Mum hates that I like Tara. I mean, she doesn't outright say it, but I can tell. And I don't blame her. Your kid isn't supposed to like her step mum.

That decides it. Tell Mum I'm dropping out. Ask her to tell Dad. When I talk to Dad, he'll already know, and Tara will be there for support... and to stop the steam coming out of Dad's ears.

It's a plan, at least.

"How was class?" Bryce asks, sliding an arm across my shoulders as we walk the cement path past the courtyard.

I shrug. "It was ok."

"Boring?" he tries.

I try a smile. "Yeah."

Bryce's popularity comes so easily to him. He was the new guy at our high school and was instantly Mr Popular. I only got in with the *it* crowd because he took an interest in me. And it happened just as easily at university. Everyone wants to be his friend. And I've seen the way other girls look at him. He'd look better with any of them, than with me.

Oh boy.

Without him, I'm a nobody. What does it mean if we actually break up? What happens to me then? Do I have friends? Do they stick around? Will I be totally ignorable?

This is why I shut him out. He can't be my rock anymore. I don't confide my fears to him because he will finally work it all out. See everything clearly. That he's too good for me. That I'm a fraud. That he should dump me immediately.

I just wasn't ready for it to happen.

Geez. Do I not trust him anymore?

I hate that.

I loved him so much the first moment I saw him. I barely spoke two words, but I was swept up in him. His name lined the margin of my notebooks. His crystal blue eyes starred in my dreams. His rosy, kissable lips filled my fantasies.

And then he was mine.

How freaking lucky am I?

I'm Bryce Kerry's girlfriend. And I've been ignoring him. I'm so messed up.

He sat by my hospital bed for weeks after the car accident. He brought my homework. He gave me foot rubs. He held me while I ugly cried.

I've shared so much with this beautiful boy, and at my lowest, I shut him out.

He deserves better.

Can I give him better?

Is it in me? Do I want to?

Why don't I want to?

I remember, with all my new scars, being so scared to be naked with him. It was scary enough at school, walking beside him with my weight gain. It was so topsy-turvy. The year prior, getting intimate worried him because he was battling an eating disorder and thought he was too skinny.

All these things brought us closer together, but now history makes me want to bolt. It feels like the problems keep mounting.

How much must we continue to share? Does our relationship have to be built on heartache? I just want the slate wiped clean.

But when I see his face, it all avalanches over me. I'll never be free of the past if I stay with him.

"Will you go on a date with me?" he asks.

It takes me by surprise. "A date?"

His smile slides left in the delicious way that always makes me melt. "Yeah. Let's do something fun."

I like the sound of fun. "What do you have in mind?"

He clasps both my hands and looks deeply into my eyes. "An arcade."

Goosebumps line my arms and a flush rises on my face like I'm fifteen again.

I giggle and nod. "Like our first date?"

"Yeah," he says with a larger-than-life grin. "Are you keen?"

"Well, I'm better at the games now. Reece taught me how to play video games. I might beat you this time."

He smirks. "*Ha*! I'd like to see you try."

I hold on to his hands tighter and I laugh.

He kisses my forehead and whispers, "It's good to hear you laugh again."

"It's good to remove the distance between us."

"Agreed."

"Do you know a good arcade close by?"

"Yeah, I checked one out not too long ago. You just let me take care of everything."

"Ok. I trust you."

"I should give you a key," Charli says, greeting me with a hug as I enter her apartment.

"*Ugh*. Another visitor," Charli's surly roommate, Naomi, says, slamming the fridge door shut. "I'm so over this."

Charli side-eyes her as she leaves for her bedroom. "Sorry, Naomi."

I swear Naomi's middle finger goes up as she leaves.

"What a bitch," I hush, rubbing a circle on Charli's back

Travis walks around from the living area. "Oh, hey, Brit," he says with a wave, trepidation in his voice.

"Hey, Travis," I say with a wave. "I didn't realise you'd be here." I sneak a look at Charli. "I can come back later. If ya want?"

Charli shakes her head, linking her arm with mine. "No way. You're always welcome."

"I can leave if you want to talk to Charli in private," Travis offers.

"No, you don't have to leave," I reply.

"It's good to see you, Brittany," Travis says, a look in his eyes like he's petrified I'm gonna scream at him or hit him until he leaves my sister alone. "It's been a long time."

"Yeah," I drawl. "I honestly didn't think I'd see you around again."

Charli and Travis share an apprehensive look.

"But I'm glad you are," I add. I send a smile Charli's way. "My sister is ecstatic you're back in her life."

Travis grins and scoops Charli's hand in his. "I feel the same way."

"You two just look so freakin cute together. How is that possible? You just got back together."

Travis smiles and sways his body to Charli's.

Charli curls her arm around Travis', and says, "Weirdly feels like no time has passed."

"Then how can it feel like it's been five years since I've seen Bryce?" I say in a frustrated rush.

The two break apart from my outburst.

"Are you sure you don't want to talk to Charli alone?" Travis says, gesturing to the front door to leave.

"No, there's so secret twin business going on," I say as we move towards the couch. "I need to talk stuff out. Another set of ears will be handy."

"Lay it on us," Charli says as she and I sit on the couch.

Travis sits by Charli's feet and looks up at me with dedication.

"He asked me on a date," I tell. Remembering it makes me smile.

"Wow, Brit. You're blushing," Charli says, giddy.

"But why weren't you smiling when you got here?" Travis asks pointedly. "Was it just the rude roommate, or were you already down?"

I bite into my lip, summoning the courage to explain.

"Just nerves?" Charli tries.

"Will you guys go with us?" I ask. "Like, a double date?"

"Don't you think you and Bryce need this time together?"

Charli counters. "Like, alone. To reconnect?"

I blow out a breath, somewhat in agreement.

"If you need us to stand with you," Travis says, meeting my eyes. "I'll be there for you."

My smile lifts. "Really?"

Charli whacks Travis' arm and her eyes slightly roll. "Well, *duh*. Of course, I'll be there if you really need me. But, I've talked to you and Bryce separately, and I really believe being alone as a couple will be beneficial."

I shrug it off. "Yeah, yeah."

"Why are you still resisting him?" Charli questions.

Travis clutches her hand. "Give her a break."

"No, it's ok," I say, defending Charli.

"I just got out of an unfulfilling relationship," Travis says softly. He clasps Charli's hand. "I was going through the motions with Sadie. I doubt I would have stayed with her, despite Charli coming back into my life, but it's hard to tell someone the truth. That you don't want to date them anymore."

Charli's eyes are sad when they meet mine. "Is that what you want?" she whispers. "To break up with Bryce?"

I sink into the couch and stare at the ceiling. "It just doesn't feel easy with him anymore. He was absolutely adorable today." I look at them, smiling. "It was like replaying when we first met. But living in the past won't keep us together. Maybe this date will help us reconnect, but... Wouldn't I go to him with my problems if I thought we had a future?"

"Yeah," Travis blurts.

Charli reaches forward and slides a hand over his mouth.

She shuts her eyes hard and whispers, "I just want you guys to work out." Her eyes open and find mine with purpose. "I'll support you in whatever you do. All I want for you is happiness."

"Breakups suck," Travis says with a huff.

"Bryce and I have already broken up twice. You'd think we'd have learnt," I joke.

"So, did you just come from talking with Bryce?" Charli asks.

"Yeah. We met up after my class finished."

"And how was school?" Charli asks reluctantly.

"I'm pretty certain I'm dropping out of uni."

"Dropping out completely," Charli questions, "or changing majors?"

"Out completely."

"*Whoah*," Charli whispers.

I take her hand and push certainty into my expression. "It's a decision. I just need the courage to put it into action."

She nods. "I'll help you every step of the way."

14

Charli

I lay back on the couch with Travis on top of me, kissing me sweetly. Brittany left for her dorm, which leaves Travis and me celebrating the fact we are officially a couple. He went through with the messy breakup, which he said took Sadie by complete surprise.

"But it was worth it," he kept repeating.

He says it's worth it to be with me.

I could not agree more.

My hands glide across the cropped sides of his hair. I smile and sigh. "D'you think you'll grow your hair out again?"

"I dunno," he says, picking up a piece of my hair that fell across my ribs. "Ever gonna go blonde again?"

"Your hair was so cute when it would curl."

"The best girl in my memories was blonde." He smiles and kisses my nose. "The worst girls were brunettes."

My nose instantly crinkles. "*Eww.* Are you saying my brown hair reminds you of GiGi?"

"You don't remind me of GiGi," he replies. "But I loved your blonde hair. That's all."

"We are starting afresh, though. Maybe we need to accept the new version of ourselves."

He smiles and sinks deeper between my legs as his hands slide from my waist to my shoulders. "I'll always accept you." He kisses my chest. "Because in your heart, you're always the same person."

"I love you, Travis."

"I love you more. I'm such an idiot for ruining things."

I shush him, lightly tapping a finger to his lips. "Don't. We can't change the past. We can just be happy we are together in the present."

"How did I get so lucky?"

"Just keep being you."

The distinct sound of keys jingling from outside the front door, sound.

Travis lifts himself up from on top of me and a slight blush coats his cheeks. "Did your roommate leave?"

"Maybe?"

The door swings open. "Charlotte?"

I suck in a breath and my stomach somersaults. I scoot my legs from around Travis and launch off the couch. Hastily, I move toward the kitchen, hoping to stop Felix from coming any closer.

Felix drops his backpack to the floor and places a six-pack of beer on the kitchen bench.

"Felix?" I say, mortified.

"Hey, how are you?" Felix says, stepping forward. His hand reaches to caress my face, his lips pout to kiss mine.

"*Ahh,*" I stammer, pulling back.

"Um, hi," Travis says, stepping behind me.

"Oh," Felix says, pulling back. He laughs and says, "Didn't realise you had company."

"Yeah," I say, chewing inside my cheek. "We were never good at that call ahead thing."

"Charli?" Travis asks hesitantly.

"Sorry mate, are you staying or going?" Felix asks, jovial in this hella-awkward moment. "Charlotte and I have this unwritten rule: we can crash at one another's places anytime we need."

"Ah, yeah, about that," I start, fidgeting with the hair that for some reason won't stay behind my ear.

"You ok?" Felix asks, running an arm around my lower back and sliding in close to me. "You look a little rattled."

"Hang on," Travis says. I turn to him and his eyes grow circular as he takes in Felix and me. "Is this a *more-than-a-friend* situation?"

My mouth opens to respond. To reassure him. To set boundaries. But nothing good comes to mind.

"Well, we are friends," Felix says, his fingers creeping down to my bum.

"Charli?" Travis' voice goes up an octave as I rush out from under Felix's arm.

I huff a sigh, and say, "Felix, you have to leave."

"What?" Felix says, blowing out a breath like he's in shock.

I run my hands up my face and scrunch them in my hair with frustration. "You have to go."

"Charlotte, we have an agreement," Felix says. "It works for us."

He takes a step forward and I take a step back, shaking my head. "Not anymore."

"No?" Felix questions. "You sure you wanna end it all? It's a two-way street, Charlotte."

Travis groans in frustration. "Dude, if you really cared for her, you'd be calling her Charli. Why don't you show her some respect and listen to what she's saying to you?"

My heartbeat slows as I listen to Travis speak. This boy is so wonderful. A small smile brightens my face and I take a step forward. "I'm sure. I'm here with Travis and *only* Travis."

Felix's eyes overgrow, and he slings his bag over his back. "Ok. If that's what you want."

He turns and walks to the door. There's nothing more I can say to him. I'm done with being used. I'm done with using others. I'd much rather be in a place where I'm working with a partner to make a healthy, loving relationship with mutual respect. I turn to Travis as Felix shuts the door behind him. I want Travis to be the person I work on a relationship with.

"I, I..." I stammer.

Travis holds his elbow, eyes on the front door. "You and he...?"

"I haven't seen him since before you and I started seeing each other." It's like I'm afraid to get too close to him.

"Any other guys like that?" He turns his face to me. "Anyone else you have an arrangement with?"

"No," I hush. "And I'll make sure everyone from my past knows I'm not available." I take a step toward him. "You're the only person I want to be with." I take his hands. "You're my number one from here on out."

Travis looks down at my hands clasping his. He looks to the door, back to me, and then smiles. "I want you too. And I don't want you to feel bad about your past. Hell, I was still dating someone the first time we slept together. I'm no saint, Charli." He squeezes my hands. "But we can work through anything. We just can't keep secrets. Not talking about our true feelings pulled us apart last time. I want this to work too. I just want you."

"Oh, Travis." I rush my arms around his neck as his arms envelope my waist. I kiss his lips with a burning passion and etch a cross into my heart, promising to make things work with this one-of-a-kind boy.

"I'm sick of all your visitors," Naomi shouts, stomping out of her bedroom. "The months you're gone don't make up for it."

"Why are you yelling?" I counter.

"I'm moving out," she blurts.

"You can't leave," I argue. "We have a lease. You'll still have to pay your share of the rent."

"Not happening. I hate living with you," she complains.

My mouth falls open, speechless.

"I'll be out by the end of the week," Naomi says, daggers in her eyes.

She stomps back into her bedroom and slams her door so hard the entire apartment quakes.

"*Bitch*," I hiss.

Travis rubs my back, searching for words of comfort, which elude him.

"It's ok," I mumble, rounding the corner and plonking on the couch.

"Did she mean that?" he asks, sitting beside me.

"Hopefully it was just her period talking."

My phone buzzes on the nearby table. I pick it up, hoping for a good distraction, and read the text message.

"It's a text from Brittany," I tell him. "She wants to go out tonight. Do you wanna hit the clubs?"

Travis smirks. "Clubbing?"

"As if you don't go out all the time."

He shrugs. "I am at uni. What else is there to do?"

"I should go. Brit and Bryce are so rocky at the moment."

"D'you think they're still going out on their date?"

I shake my head, reading her three text messages. "The arcade date will be next week, they haven't picked a day. Bryce is going out with her, purely because Brittany wants out of the dorms."

"You think they'll be ok together?"

"She was so hot and cold talking about him. Then there's the decision to leave uni, which I don't think she's told Bryce."

Travis clasps my hand, and asks, "You want to go together? We can keep an eye on them while also keeping a distance."

I kiss his cheek and smile. "That sounds wonderful. I'm still hopeful they'll work through their issues."

"Yeah. They've been together forever."

I wrap my arms around his neck, loving the concern in his eyes.

"Plus, we can celebrate our relationship," I say. "Have a fun night, feeling all official and stuff."

He laughs, wrapping his arms around me. "Official and stuff? Sure, let's do it."

I cheer and smooch him.

"I'll need to go home and change," he says. "Should I come back here to leave with you?"

"Brittany and Bryce will be at the dorms. I'll go there so we can all leave together."

"Deal."

After finding my tightest, jaw-dropping outfit to impress the pants off Travis, I fix my hair in a high ponytail and add some eyeliner and dark lipstick. I finish a beer Felix had left behind, and pick up my phone to drop it into my clutch purse, when I notice a text. I assume it's from Kumi. We were texting as I got ready for tonight.

Kumi is so adorable. She started dating a girl who works with her, and was terrified to tell me in case I was pining for her. After ensuring Kumi I'm happy for her, I sent a happy snap of me and Trav. Kumi sent photos of her and her girlfriend, and I swear she's dating a runway model. If I were Kumi, I'd pick her too. *Ha*, I'm sure she has a great personality too.

I open the message and it's from Travis.

> *(Travis)* Something's come up and I'm gonna have to meet you guys later.
>
> *(Me)* I can wait for you.
>
> *(Travis)* Sadie wants to talk. It's about our breakup. I just want to get it over with so we can move on.

Shit.

> *(Me)* Ok. Text me when you're done and I'll let you know where we are.
>
> *(Travis)* Will do. Thank you and sorry.
>
> *(Me)* No problem.

Big problem.

Ugh.

Really? He's hanging out with his ex-girlfriend instead of coming out with me? This sucks.

I buckle my high, strappy stilettos, and leave for the next bus to the university.

"Where's Travis?" Brit asks when we meet by her door.

"He's going to meet us later."

"Uh, ok?"

"The most awkward, cringe-worthy thing happened earlier."

Her eyes widen. "Tell me."

"Travis and I were fooling around at my place, and Felix walked in."

She shoves me as she gasps. "Get out! Are you serious? What did you do?"

"It was a nightmare."

"What did Travis say? *Ohmigawd.* Is that why he's not here?"

I raise my hands to halt her rushing questions. "No. Travis and I are cool." One big, deep breath in. "He's meeting up with his ex."

Brittany's jaw drops. "What? How are you not freaking out?"

"Because I trust him. He understood everything with Felix, so I'm doing the same for him."

"So, why is he seeing her?"

I shrug. "Something about their breakup. I'm sure he'll tell me when he meets up with us later."

Brittany's smile is sympathetic as she rubs my arm.

"Seriously, Brit. I'm fine."

"Ok." She half believes me.

"Hey, Charli," Bryce calls, walking the hall and waving.

"Hey," I reply.

He lands by us and gives me a hug. "Good to see you."

"You too," I say, as we pull out of the hug.

Bryce turns to Brittany and wraps his arms around her. As he kisses her cheek, I notice her lack of affection towards him.

C'mon, Brit.

Bryce turns to me, ignoring Brittany's coldness.

"I remember when you'd go to parties in ripped jeans and old band t-shirts," Bryce jokes. "I mean, you're still a badass. All those tattoos."

"Too much?"

Bryce smiles and shakes his head. "You look more like yourself than ever."

"Thank you, Bryce. I appreciate it."

Brittany huffs, clasping her hands in front. "Well, shall we go? Or do you two besties wanna keep chatting here in the hall?"

"Brit," I hush. The tension is ice cold.

Bryce holds out his hand towards her. "I'm happy to go."

Brittany's jaw clenches, and she takes Bryce's hand like it's a mandatory requirement.

I follow behind them, wishing I had waited for Travis instead of leaving with The Frosty Pair.

"You look really beautiful tonight, Brittany," Bryce says, giving her hand a gentle swing.

"Thanks," she mumbles.

Oh boy. Do we need drinks, or what?

We take a train into central station, and thankfully we can use the whooshing of travel as an excuse not to talk. The carriage is crowded, so we huddle by the rails. When a seat is free, we urge Brittany to take it in case the train jerks and she lands awkwardly on her bad hip and knee.

Brittany takes a seat and whips out her phone. When she's distracted by the screen, I scoot closer to Bryce.

"How are you doing?" I ask him.

He blows out a breath. "Fine, I guess."

I'm deflated. "You don't sound confident."

His head leans against the rail as he takes another exhausted breath.

"You and Brit..." I start the sentence, but looking between the two of them, I don't see the point in answering it.

"Brittany said you're back with Travis."

I smile. "Yeah."

"How's that going?"

"Really well. I'm really happy."

"Wasn't he supposed to come with us?"

"He is. He will be," I stumble with my words. "He's just late."

"And you're not worried that the past will repeat itself?"

I suck in a breath. Like the fact he's hanging out with his ex-girlfriend instead of being here with me?

His eyes search mine. "What? What is it? You look freaked."

I shake my head. "No. I'm cool. Everything's ok."

He doesn't buy it.

I sigh and then blurt, "He's with his ex."

Apprehension covers his expression.

"He's committed to me," I defend.

"Just be careful," Bryce warns. "After everything with me and Brit, I don't want it to be your turn in relationship hell."

That last word strikes me. "*Hell*? You think it is *hell* with Brittany?"

"I dunno. I wish she'd open up to me."

"Did something happen over the past months to cause a rift between you two?"

He shakes his head. "I don't think so. Maybe she should have had a gap year? I can tell she struggled to adapt to uni life. Like, maybe the wrong major?"

"You two never discuss it?"

"It's not the first time she's cut off communication with me."

It takes me aback. "Whaddaya mean?"

"It was the same in high school. She forced us into a break because she couldn't talk to me. She accused me of wanting to be with Chloe Benson or wanting to dump her because she walked with a cane. I never said or thought any of those things, but she decided they were true." He rubs between his eyes, wincing. "Shit, what does she think I say about her now?"

"Oh, Bryce. I'm so sorry."

He looks me square in the eyes, and all I see is pain. "She thinks she holds me back. All I've done is love her."

"She loves you too."

He looks over his shoulder, watching her scroll on her phone. His shoulders droop, and he says, "I just want her to be happy."

Later at the club, on my third vodka and tonic, Brittany slurps back her vodka raspberry and slams down the glass.

"Come dance with me," Brittany says, curling her arm around mine and gesturing to the dancefloor.

"Ok." I look around her. "Should we tell Bryce?"

"He's fine," she blurts. "Come dance."

"Ok." I let her lead me to the dancefloor. I spy over the top of her as my high heels make me a couple of inches taller than my identical sister. Her hips sashay as we push through to the middle of the dancefloor. My smile grows as she dances. Seeing her hips shimmy makes my heart warm because she's obviously in no pain.

Brittany twists around, holding my hand high and dancing in close to me. Holding my drink steady, I wrap an arm around her and as we bump side to side. She giggles and steps wider. She dances away from me, relaxed, mixing in with other people, and having fun.

My anxiety gets the better of me, and I move in closer to her. Brittany has been such a loose cannon lately. I can't assume she's ok. She will seem fine, and the next moment she flies off the handle. In a ball of tears, or struggling against a blade.

Wow. I cannot let that happen again.

I spy Bryce through a group of people. He's chatting with two guys I assume are his mates from uni. I pan across the bar and crane my neck to view the front doors. I want Travis to walk through so badly.

As Brittany and I leave the dancefloor, I pull her by an empty booth.

"Have you told Bryce about dropping out of school?"

"No. Don't you dare blab."

"I wasn't going to."

"Then why do you care?"

"I'm just trying to gauge your communication levels."

Brittany *tsks* and rolls her eyes. "Charli, just because you and Travis are back together, doesn't make you a relationship expert. Two seconds ago you were a polyamorist."

"But I was honest with everyone I dated."

"Dating?" she says it like it's a big joke. "Be real. You were having casual sex."

"You still think I'm a slut?" the hurt radiates off every syllable.

"I didn't say that."

"Why are you trying to hurt me? I'm here to support you."

"You're acting like you're better than me."

I throw a hand up to block the view of her face. "I don't need this right now."

I turn and walk away before I say anything I'll regret. I walk outside the club and the fresh, chilled air hits me like a slap in the face.

I want to scream in Brittany's face. Somehow we are fifteen again and acting like enemies. It had better be depression turning her into a bitch. I can't rebuild our relationship again. It was too much work. I don't have the strength to do it again.

I sit against the outside wall of the club and check my phone. Still no text from Travis.

He said he'd be here. He has to be here soon.

I hope nothing has happened to him on the way here. What if I'm here drinking and he's been in a traumatic accident? What if he needs my help?

Or what if he's in bed with Sadie? What if she convinced him being with her is where he ought to be? What if she's won him over?

And I've lost him again?

I take another large mouthful of vodka and tonic.

"Hey, you ok?" Bryce asks, crouching beside me.

I try my best reassuring smile. "Yeah, I'm cool. Just waiting for Travis."

Bryce sighs and then takes a long sip of his drink.

I bite my lip and my insides flip. "Are you ok?"

He looks at me with melancholy eyes. "Do you ever get sick of waiting?"

Ok, stomach, please settle down. "Whaddaya mean?"

"We are both sitting here, waiting for someone to notice us." Another big sip. "Don't you get tired? Man, I'm tired."

"Bryce, she's not doing well. You know what it's like."

"I remember what it was like to tell her my problems and let her help me. She won't even let me listen."

"I'm sorry. If I could fix it, I would."

He rubs my arm. "I just don't want you to be sad. I don't want you waiting for some guy, who's paying more attention to somebody else. You deserve better. Actually, you deserve the best."

"They just broke up. It's complicated. I know he'll explain everything."

"Keep making excuses, and you'll get tired." He stands and holds out his hand to me. "I'm going back in. You coming?"

I inhale deeply. "I'm gonna text him. I'll be in soon."

He nods with a limp smile. As Bryce returns inside the club, I pick up my phone to my silent text chain with Travis.

(Me) Can I come over?

(Travis) Of course. Shit. I'm sorry.

(Me) Are you ok? I was worried about you.

(Travis) It was a fucking awful night. Sorry, I should have called or something.

Gulp.

My heart plummets.

My heart pitter-patters and tingles run down my spine.

He wants to see me. My breathing is rapid as I move toward the taxi line.

I quickly text Brittany that I'm leaving to see Travis. I'll be at the dorms if she needs me. I trust Bryce to ensure she gets home safe.

Travis wants to see me now. I interlace my fingers and clamp down hard, my knuckles whitening as the rest of my hands redden. That has to be good. This has to be a good thing.

Shit.

What happened to him?

A fucking awful night.

My poor Travis. What has happened to him? What am I walking into? Has he been in a fight? Is he hurt? He wasn't drinking? But what kept him away?

He was with Sadie.

He's decided to leave me to go back to her? That's the awful part. The awful part is coming. He's going to break up with me. Already. For her. To go back to her.

Shit.

Why am I going over now? My night was bad enough. Now I'm making it so much worse.

Shit.

Why would he break up with me at three-thirty in the morning? This can't be a good thing. Why does he need to do this now?

Wait, stop it, Charli.

I rub the vodka headache from my temples.

He wants to see you, you dumb girl. Stop reading into subtext that isn't there. He wants to see you. He needs you. It'll be ok.

Oh, please, let it all be ok.

I walk to his dormitory and a couple, who are leaving, let me inside. My stomach scrambles on the way to his room. Through my breaths, I summon all my courage to knock on his door.

Footsteps sound inside and then the door pulls open. His face is drained of colour and his lips draw down. His eyes are dull with fading streaks of red.

"Trav," I hush, running a hand along the side of his face. "My goodness, what's happened?"

His jaw flexes, and he sniffs back what sounds like the remnants of tears. He takes my hand and pulls me in.

He closes the door and lets out a shattered sigh. "I don't know where to begin."

He sits on his bed, resting his head in his hands, and hunched over bent knees. I sit beside him and rub a circle on his back.

I wait for him to speak. The horrible silence brings thoughts of an impending breakup, but I quickly erase it from my mind when I watch his hunched body. I don't think this is about me at all. Something terrible has happened to *him*.

Shit. What on Earth could it be?

"You don't have to talk about it if you don't want to," I offer. "If it's too personal or something."

Travis lifts his head and wraps his arms around me. He breathes heavily against the nape of my neck, and I press my hands into his back.

I have to ask it. "This isn't about us, is it?"

He sighs, and in a wavering voice, replies, "I don't know."

I gulp loudly as I hold him against me.

"I hope not," he whispers.

What does that mean? I can't bring myself to ask it aloud.

Travis pulls away from me and rubs his palms over his eyes. "It's Sadie."

I rub against the pang in my heart. I bite inside my lip hard.

He groans in pain and doubles over. "Oh, fuck."

"Holy crap, Travis," I gasp and rush off the bed to kneel in front of him. I hold on to his thighs and search for his eyes. "Baby, what's happened?"

He moves his hands, and tears streak his cheeks. "She's

pregnant.”

I let him go and my bum hits the carpet. “Oh... ok...”

He swipes his eyes. “What am I supposed to do?”

I rub my lips together and eye the floor as I ask, “Are you going back to her?”

“I don’t want to,” he says, and I look up. “Does that make me an awful person? Because I still don’t want to be with her?”

“No,” I say, standing on my knees. I run my hands along the sides of his face and press my forehead against his. “No, you’re not awful. It’s a big shock. You’re allowed to not know what to do.”

His hands creep around the small of my back and his sigh is less defeated. “I’m sorry I didn’t call you sooner.”

“How long have you known? Have you been alone this whole time, dealing with this?”

“Pretty much. I just felt blank.”

I kiss his cheek. “I’m here for you.”

He kisses my lips, soft and slow. “Thank you. I love you. So much.”

“*Geez.*” I let out a relieved breath. “I was so worried you were breaking up with me.”

“I told you that will never happen.”

I kiss him again. “Good, because I need you. I love you so much.”

“A baby,” he whispers.

“Is she sure?”

“What?”

“Is she sure? Has she gone to the doctor?”

His hands run down my back as I watch his frown. "I don't know. She just said she took a test, and it was positive."

"She didn't show you?"

His eyebrows raise. "You think she's faking?"

I shake my head. "No, I'm just saying it could be a false positive. Don't get too stressed out. A blood test could prove she's not pregnant."

"Really? The tests aren't always right?"

I smile at the hopefulness brightening his face. "No. Nothing is bulletproof. Don't jump to the worst-case scenario until it's confirmed. Did she mention going to a doctor?"

He pulls me onto his lap and cuddles me. "Charli, I don't really know. There was just a lot of yelling."

"Yelling?"

"She was basically screaming at me. I wouldn't be surprised if the whole dorm knows she's pregnant."

"Wow. Why would she yell about it?"

"I think because I didn't give her the reaction she wanted. She expected me to say we'd get back together."

"Oh, that figures."

"But why should I be unhappy with her? Wouldn't that make the baby unhappy too?"

I nod. "I would think so. You don't want a messed up kid like I was growing up. Trying to impress a dad that was never fully present. Mum and Dad should have divorced so I could have adjusted. Instead, I tried holding them together despite their relationship being over."

"You really see it like that now?"

I cuddle into him. "I've gained a lot of perspective since high school."

"I reckon I didn't help with that."

I smirk. "Yeah, not really."

"I don't want to be that jerk again. What are people gonna say when they find out Sadie's pregnant and I'm not sticking by her?"

"You're not abandoning her. Of course, you'll help her. You can help her without being in a romantic relationship."

"Mmm, I guess that's true."

"Wouldn't people prefer to see you in a loving relationship?"

He smiles and kisses my cheek. "Yeah. You're totally right."

I turn to meet his lips and kiss him hard. "I'm sticking with you," I say. "I'll help you however I can."

"I love you, beautiful girl."

"I love you, my one and only."

He hushes a laugh. "I like that one."

"Good, cause it's true."

"Sorry, I scared you. The last thing I wanted was you thinking I was breaking up with you."

"It's all fine now."

"Are you staying with me tonight?"

I straddle his hips. "I'm not going anywhere."

He looks me up and down, grinning. "Why do you look like a bombshell tonight?"

"I was planning on seducing you."

He squeezes my bum. "It's certainly attention-grabbing."

"You wanna see how fast it can hit the floor?"

His lips twist with worry. "I'd love to, but I'm still rattled."

"That's ok. I understand." A baby? A fucking baby?

My phone dings in my purse.

"That might be Brit," I say, reaching for my phone.

(Brittany) I'm sorry for being an uber bitch.

I grin and breathe out a layer of tension that was building inside me.

(Me) You're more than forgiven. Sorry for being controlling. Get home safe.

(Brittany) I love you.

(Me) xoxo

15

Brittany

"Brittany," Bryce says over the music, taking my hand. "Let's go, ok?"

I frown as I twist a heel on the sticky bar floor. I pan across the sea of partying people and badly want to vanish between them. My body sways to the rhythm of alcohol flooding my veins. I gaze at the hazy, foggy version of him, and his eyes become clear. The more I look into those crystal eyes that stole my heart years ago, my head clears. I blink until I'm looking at this boy for the first time all over again.

"Ok," I say.

He leads me by the hand out of the bar, through the crowd of people, and I watch the flex between his shoulder blades.

I squeeze around his knuckles as my balance wobbles. I trip

through the doorway as the chill of the night air frazzles my skin. My stomach flips when I realise Bryce is dragging me along, keeping a step ahead.

We wait in line for a taxi, and he releases my hand. I swallow slowly and hug my waist, busying myself by watching the people line up behind us. All of whom are having more fun than we are.

Bryce turns and looks me up and down. He takes a step closer, and asks, "Are you cold?"

I shake my head. "I'm ok."

He drapes an arm around my shoulders nonetheless and briskly rubs my arm. Now I feel the sprouting goosebumps I was too distracted to notice before. Even though Bryce is caring towards me, there's still an undeniable shift in our demeanours. Like we'd both prefer to be anywhere else.

We hold hands in the back seat of the taxi, but it's limp at best. There's so much distance between us, whereas in the past we'd try to cram both our bodies into one seat in a fit of giggles.

It hasn't been like that in a long time.

"Did you have a nice night?" he asks, walking me to my dorm room, his hands in his pockets.

"Yeah," I say, unlocking my door. "I tried to have fun."

He smiles. It's weak but genuine. "That's good, Britty."

I smile at him and step inside. "You coming in?"

He nods. "Yeah."

Bryce follows me in and I snatch a makeup wipe from a drawer and perch on the edge of my bed. He takes a step forward and then back before moving over to the bed and sitting beside me.

"We've stopped talking," he says.

Somehow it feels like a bullet wound to the chest.

It's true... but I don't like hearing the words come from his lips.

His hand slips over mine and then dashes it away. After a deep breath, he says, "We're bad together."

A gasp shoots out of me. "What?"

His eyes gleam with sadness. "It's my fault. I stopped checking in on you and we drifted apart."

I clench my jaw and look at the picture collage of our relationship on my wall. "You're not the one at fault. I stopped talking to you."

"It's not good, Brit."

"I know. I know."

"Do you even want to be with me anymore?"

I close my eyes tight and hush, "Please don't ask me that."

"Does that mean no?"

"Bryce."

"I've been trying so hard to be happy this year. To make up for all the hurt that happened during high school. But I've been trying to do it all on my own."

"I don't know what it's like to be on my own. It's been you and me for so long."

"Be honest, Brittany, do you still want to be with me?"

Tears roll down my cheeks. "No." I face him. "No. I want to break up."

He draws in a breath as tears break from his eyes. He nods.

"Ok."

"I don't know who I am," I say. "I'm your girlfriend, or I'm the girl with the limp. I want a new identity. I want an identity period."

Bryce runs a hand along my cheek and into my hair. "I still love you." He kisses me. "I'm just not in love anymore."

I clutch his wrist and nod as our foreheads rest together. "I feel the same. I'll always love you. But we aren't *us* anymore."

Like magnets, we cling to each other. Our hearts beat wildly and our bodies tremble. He kisses my neck, and I know what will happen tonight will be for the last time.

His hands run down my back and I shiver in the best way. A breathy moan escapes my lips. I suck on the curve of his collarbone. His hand slides inside my skirt and I smile as he cups my bum.

My hands run inside his shirt and pull it up to his torso, and eventually over his head. Our lips press together as I undo his fly.

As our lips part, and his breath tickles my ear. His hands take over my body. He cups my breasts and in one more action my top hits the floor.

I unhook the clasps of my bra with anticipation. I need this so badly. I need his body before it truly sinks in this is over.

That it is ok it's over.

The last of our clothing hits the floor, and I lay on top of him. Our last few times I was always underneath. We just went through the motions. Almost lifeless. Like it was a chore to do. Somehow this time I am filled with confidence. I sit against him and grin, running my hands under my breasts and then down onto his body.

He feels wonderful inside me. A perfect fit. It's like we can get this back one day. If by some long shot we're making a big mistake.

Is this a mistake? Should I always be with him?

He smiles at me and draws a finger under my chin. The way his head tilts confirms it is ok we end this. We will always have memories of what was. And we will always be best friends.

In the morning, we wake up, wrapped together. My hand runs against the side of his face as his eyes slowly open.

"Hey," he whispers, smiling.

I smile back. "Hey."

"Thanks for last night," he says, nuzzling his face by mine.

"Last night was perfect."

His hand sits against my lower back and I close my eyes, pretending for one moment that this isn't a breakup.

I open my eyes, and his face morphs into apprehension.

"You ok?" I ask in a flat tone.

"I'm fine. Are you?"

I nod. "Yep."

A worried look crosses his face. "Should I go?"

His hands leave my body.

I nod. "I think so."

He kisses my forehead. "You're still important to me, Brittany. Please call me if you ever need anything."

As he sits up, I take his hand and interlace our fingers, and say, "You're important to me too. Take your meds when you need to and if you ever feel yourself slipping and need someone to talk to, you call me. I don't want anything bad to ever happen to you."

"You've been the most awesome best friend a person could ask for."

He kisses my cheek, and my body relaxes.

"You've been a great rock. But we need to find ourselves on our own," I say.

He moves out of bed and gets dressed. "Thanks, Brit."

My heart warms. "Thanks, Bryce."

When he leaves, I flop onto the bed and spread out like a starfish. I breathe out a long breath like I've been holding onto it for a year.

It's done.

It's done and I'm ok. I'm me. I'm me and I'm ok.

Relief.

I should have a *me* day. Go out for great coffee and a fully loaded breakfast. Maybe a little retail therapy? I still need the perfect pair of ballet flats to go with that pink polka dot dress I bought in Paris. Maybe today is the perfect day to debut wearing that dress. A dress to celebrate me. Being on my own and ok with it.

Charli will want an update, but I want to mull it over first. I need a cinnamon-dusted cappuccino STAT. Time to think on my next move. Time to discover what will bring me a boatload of happiness. That coffee sounds better and better.

I throw on the nearest t-shirt and shorts, and move to the

showers to wash off last night and start fresh. I breathe out one more moment of relief. Everything will be ok from here on out. Bryce was never the problem. He didn't cause me to feel alone or stressed or sad. We just disconnected. We need time to find ourselves. To have adventures. To be individuals and happy.

After my shower, I return to my room and turn the music up. I stream an upbeat party playlist and dance like nobody's watching. I catch myself in the mirror a few times and laugh. The dimples in my skin and the scars don't matter. It's time for sun. It's time to forget what others think. More precisely, wondering and inventing what others think about me. Not once over the last year have I considered my own opinion. It's all about outside influences and their opinions.

It stops today.

I hold on to that magical moment in Paris. Staring at the couture designs in the boutique window. Fashion, beauty, dreams. I want to multiply that single moment. I want it in abundance in my life.

I get dressed in my polka dot dress and place a sketchbook on my desk. There's a reason I packed it from home. Design has never left my heart, even though my brain shut it out. I stare at the blank page and pick up a baby-doll shade of nail polish that matches my dress. In long, careful strokes, I coat each nail, and my mind leisurely works on what to fill the page. As my nails dry, I turn to the mirror. I tussle out my hair and observe the shade.

It'd be nice to go blonder. A brighter shade.

I flick on my hair straightener. It's been so long since I styled my hair, and the flat iron will help it shine.

I pick up my phone and text Charli. Last night, she said she's staying with Travis, so she might be still on campus.

> **(Me) Can you send me the contact info for your hairstylist? I want to get my hair coloured.**

I sit at my desk and contemplate my next text. It will be to Mum. Telling her I'm coming home and need to talk. I need to word it so she won't get anxious that something is wrong. I also need her to know I'm being serious. That she needs to be home to actively listen to me. Not wrapped up in work calls or trying to push me into taking over her career.

As I blow over my nails, I look at the text chain with Charli. It's weird she hasn't responded already. Since that day at *Sully's*, I haven't had to wait long for her replies. We've been inseparable since that day.

What happened last night? I scrunch my eyes tight, thinking through my vodka amnesia to recall memories.

She went to see Travis... Because Travis didn't come out like he said... She kept waiting for him... She left to find him...

Shit.

Did they break up last night?

Oh boy. She's head over heels about him. It would just crush her.

Geez. She's a rebound chick. He used her. I knew I should have been mad at him! I should never have trusted him after everything he put her through in high school.

I'm going to kill him!

I pick up my phone, manicure be damned, and call Charli. It rings out for the first time, and on my second panic-stricken ring, she answers.

"Hey," she says flatly.

"Charli, what's going on? Are you ok?" I say in a rush.

"Yeah, yeah," she says, the hangover thick in her voice. "Sorry, I didn't look at my phone before. I can text you the phone number."

I *tsk*. "No. I don't care about the hairstylist. You and Travis. Are you ok? What was his excuse for ditching you last night?"

She blows out a hard breath, which distorts through the phone.

"Charli?"

"He's sleeping. I'll meet you somewhere for coffee."

"*Apricot Café*," I suggest, now knowing she's still on campus. "I've been dying for a cinnamon cappuccino all morning."

"Ok," she says, trying to sound bright, yet her tone is still defeated. "I'll be there in like fifteen."

"Ok. See you then."

Shit. She sounds horrible. But she's still at his place? So, they didn't break up? But Bryce was in my bed and we broke up.

Ohmigawd. I forgot Bryce and I broke up. *Ha!* Ok, I'm keen for her drama if it distracts me from my own.

"Charli?" I grimace as we meet outside *Apricot Café*. "You look like hell."

Her eye makeup sits under her eyes in faded black from a lazy attempt at washing her face. Her dark hair is wild with frizz, and her clothes are sizes too big and hang off her skinny frame.

"Forgive me for having a hangover," she grizzles.

"I'm sorry, it's just such a difference from the bombshell look from last night."

She shrugs, her face drooping. "I didn't want to walk around campus in that outfit." She looks me in the eye and her lips twist. "Some might say it was slutty."

"I'm sorry," I blurt and grab her shoulders. "I didn't mean it. I was angry at myself and took it on you. I don't think you're a slut."

Just a rebound chick.

Gah! Brittany, stop being a mega bitch!

Her smile is limp as she pulls at the baggy t-shirt. "I just threw on something of Travis'. I'll pick up my dress later."

"Are you and he good?"

I brace for the answer.

She sighs and smooths back her hair. "Yeah. There's just a lot of new information."

"He was keeping stuff from you?"

She shakes her head. "No, it was news to him." She gasps. "Man, I forgot. I totally ditched you last night? What happened with you and Bryce?"

I chew my lip, searching for the most delicate way to word it.

Charli blinks and sizes me up. "Um, you look drop-dead-gorgeous. Like, you're reinvented or something. So, it was a good night?"

Her smile illuminates her face, ridding some of the hangover mood killer.

"Hard to say exactly. Yes, in a lot of ways, but..."

"Brit?"

"Let's get a table. Sounds like we both have a lot to reveal."

After we find a table and order our coffees, I have to ask, "Did you and Travis breakup last night?"

"No way," she says defiantly. "It did terrify me when I thought I was walking into a breakup. Thankfully, it wasn't. If anything, we're more committed than ever."

I sit back in my chair, relieved and surprised. "Really? So, what happened?"

She slides her hands over her face, shaking her head in disbelief. "I don't know how to say it."

"It's to do with the ex-girlfriend?"

Charli looks like she's gonna hurl. Her face greens as she nods.

I lean forward, my mind whirring. "What is it? If you two didn't break up, then why does his ex matter?"

Charli sucks in her bottom lips and her eyes round. Desperation soaks into her face as she wants to tell me, but just can't say it aloud.

Charli and Travis. Still Together. Ex-girlfriend. Feeling sick. Travis not coming out. Charli staying with him. My mind hurries to calculate what all these things mean when placed together.

Light bulb.

My mouth falls open as I stare at Charli. She swallows

roughly, sitting up and staring at me with pleading eyes.

I whisper harshly, "Is she pregnant?"

Tears spring from Charli's eyes, and she's quick to cover them with her palms.

My hands clasp over my face as my breathing intensifies. "Oh shit," I gasp in a muffle.

We stare at each other, long and hard, in silence. The tension breaks when our coffees arrive. The server is quick to leave, probably debating whether we are having a fight or gossiping about last night.

"What are you going to do?" It's the only thing I can think to ask.

The pleading doesn't leave her face, but bravery breaks through. "Stay with him," she admits.

"Do you think you can?"

A tear rolls down her cheek as she whispers, "I love him."

I leave my seat and give her a hug. She latches on like it's going to fix everything.

"It sucks," she whispers into my neck.

I rub her back. "I know."

I return to my seat and show her a sympathetic smile.

A baby? That's too huge.

"Distract me," she says, fidgeting in her seat. "Tell me about your night."

I take a long sip of coffee and reflect on all the good feelings I wanted this morning.

"What happened with you and Bryce?" she elaborates as I place the cup down.

I clear my throat and avert my eyes from hers.

"Oh no," she hesitates. "You didn't."

I flick my eyes to hers. She's figured it out.

She pouts, her shoulders drooping. "You broke up?"

I smile, and it's not painful. "Yeah."

Charli covers her face with her hands and cries, "I'm so sorry. I'm such a bitch. I make everything about me."

"What? Don't be sorry. That was huge news."

She pats her face dry, last night's makeup looking more hellish, and says, "I should have been more concerned about you and Bryce. We've been talking about it for so long, and when it really goes south, I concentrate on my new relationship."

"You wouldn't fix it. The break up was inevitable."

"I could have helped you."

"It was mutual."

"What?"

"Bryce and I agreed on it. He was the one to suggest it first."

Charli sits back in surprise. "Really?"

My smile grows. "We are ok. Bryce stayed the night. It was wonderful, and we agree we will always be friends."

"Wow. That does sound great."

I nod. "I'm happy."

Charli smiles. "That's all I want for you."

"It's all I want for you, too. Is staying with Travis, who is going to be a father... *Ohmigawd.* That's insane... Is staying with him despite all that, going to make you happy?"

She nods with conviction. "Yes. It will."

"Have you thought it all through? You *just* found out."

"I'm not leaving him. He did nothing wrong."

"He cheated on his pregnant girlfriend."

Disgust colours Charli's face and instant regret sours my stomach.

"He didn't know about the baby," Charli says, anger reddening her face. "I can't explain how right our first night together felt. It was meant to be. We *are* meant to be."

I reach a hand across. "I'll support you all the way."

"I'm not a slut and he's not a monster."

"I know. I'm sorry. I feel sick over saying those things." I swallow hard and shake my head. "I remember the first time I was called a slut. It was by Chloe Benson in front of the entire cheer squad and football team. I know how horrible it is to hear, and I should stop saying it."

Charli latches onto my hand. "I forgive you."

I sigh out in relief. "Thank you."

"I'm overly sensitive to it because when you date both girls and guys you hear it way too often, despite all my relationships being consensual."

The heat in my cheeks expands. "I had no idea. I promise not to say the word again."

She smiles. "Thanks Brit."

"I've got your back, no matter what you decide to do next."

16

Charli

I fix my high bun atop my head and roll my sleeves down as I walk into work. My neck is strained and I've had little sleep with everything that's going on. Brittany and Bryce are over, and I'm back with my one true love whose ex-girlfriend is pregnant.

Why must everything be such a nightmare?

"Hey Mike," I say in a yawn, as I place my bag in the storeroom.

"Wait," Mike says, gesturing to the bag. "Charli, can you come back to the office with me?"

"Sure. Now?"

"Yeah." He nods at the bag. "Bring that with you."

My forehead crinkles, and I shrug, picking up my bag. "Ok?"

I follow Mike into the back office, and Arthur is behind the desk. The owner. He's barely ever here as he has five different businesses he moves between.

"Hi Arthur," I say.

"Hi Charli. Take a seat," Arthur says. He's not super friendly, but that's not unlike him. He's a super busy person who gets too focused on work to smile at you.

"Everything ok?" I ask as Mike silently stands behind me and Arthur shuffles papers around his desk.

"We need to let you go," Arthur states.

My jaw drops. "What?"

"You've dropped too many shifts," Mike says. The emotion in his voice is sympathetic.

Unlike Arthur, who is still more invested in paperwork than breaking it to me gently.

I pivot between Mike and Arthur, computing if this is real. "I always work my butt off when I'm here."

"Normally," Arthur says with a nod. "But then you went on another overseas trip without notice, and you keep boycotting your shifts. We can't afford having you on the roster if you will not show up."

"My sister needed me," I plead. "She wasn't well."

"I'm sorry, Charli," Mike says, patting my shoulder. "I'd love to keep you on my crew, but you're not a team player anymore."

With that, I'm standing. "I'm trying. I just got swept up in some family stuff. I'll make it up, I swear. I need this job. Please. Arthur, Mike, please."

Arthur holds up a piece of paper. "Here's a letter of employment separation you can file with social services."

I take the letter, gobsmacked. They want me to go on unemployment payments?

"I'm fired?" It's like an anvil has fallen on me.

"Effective immediately," Arthur says.

"I'll walk you out," Mike offers.

Screw this.

I hurry out of the office and run through the bar, avoiding other staff as they say hello to me.

When I hit the street, I'm still running. I don't want to stop because then it will really sink in I was fired. I don't have a job. I'm a worthless piece of shit.

I don't let the tears fall on the way home. I unlock the front door of my apartment, to the distinct sounds of packing. Masking tape tearing, boxes folding, and clothes stuffed into bags.

I slam the front door shut, unable to go inside.

Naomi is moving out.

I'm unemployed.

I have to pay double the rent.

I have no income.

I'm screwed.

Animalistically, a scream gurgles out of me. I kick the door and escape into the elevator.

I hate this.

With trembling fingers, I call Travis' phone.

After three rings, he answers. "Hey, what's up?"

"Can I see you?" I blurt, trying to keep the emotion out of my voice.

"Yeah, sure. I thought you had a shift now."

No luck, a sob barges out of me.

"*Whoah.* Baby, are you ok?"

"I need to see you," I whimper, trying to rid my tears.

"I'll come to your place."

"No. Can I go to yours?"

"Sure. I'll get back there now."

"Thank you."

"Are you all right? Where are you?"

"I'm on my way." I can't explain this over the phone. I'll completely fall apart. "See you soon."

"Ok. I'll meet you in front of the dorms."

On campus, Travis meets me before I get to the dorms and scoops me in his arms.

"I could hear it in your voice," he whispers by my ear. "What's happened?"

I hold on to him like he's a life raft and I'm amidst a turbulent sea.

He walks me to his room, and when I sit on his bed, I still can't speak.

Travis strokes my cheek and tilts my chin up. "Is it us? I understand if you're scared. It will be difficult."

I shut my eyes and turn my head away. Why is everything a nightmare?

He whispers, "I won't hold it against you if you want to break up."

My posture shatters and I throw my limp body against him. With all my strength, I wrap my arms around him as my face burrows into his chest.

"I need you," is all I have the energy to say.

He rubs my back vigorously. "I'm here. You've got me. Can you talk about it?"

I inhale deeply, and on the exhale, look up into his beautiful dark eyes. "I got fired."

His mouth falls open, and his eyes droop. "Shit. Really? Why?"

"Because I chose Brittany over work." It comes out childish. I want to blame Arthur and Mike, and not take responsibility. I wouldn't redo the last few weeks any other way. There were no other options.

I had to do what I did.

Travis takes me into his room, continuing to comfort me as he says, "Baby, I'm sorry. Did they give you a notice period?"

"They used the words *effective immediately.*"

"Shit. Can your parents help you out with rent money in the meantime?"

"*Ha!*" I blurt.

Travis blinks at me.

I shake my head. "Sorry. It's just, my parents refuse to support me."

"Refuse?"

"When I left school, they turned their backs on me."

"Over a high school certificate?" Travis' face screws up. "Lord, get over it. It's not like you're a bum on the couch. You've been working, volunteering, and living your life. Is it seriously just because of school?"

I shrug. "As soon as I brought up the conversation about dropping out, they both said they didn't support my decision. I had to move in with Reece because I couldn't live with Mum."

Travis is silent as he draws a slow circle on my back.

I chew inside my cheek as I watch his mind whirring.

"D'you think they're holding a grudge because I took drugs?" I ask.

He snaps out of his trance and finds my eyes. "I wasn't thinking that."

I rest my head on his shoulder. "I don't think Mum or Dad has ever truly forgiven me."

"What made you turn to drugs in the first place?" Travis whispers. "I know Kellie died, but was it because you didn't have anyone to talk to?"

"Kellie was who I talked to."

"That makes sense," he says, defeat in his tone. "I wish we were still together back then. I'm so mad at myself for not being there for you. I really thought the people in your life would take care of you."

"Don't beat yourself up. I wouldn't have let you in."

"Maybe you would have if we never broke up. I hate that I took advantage of you."

I gently shush him. "Don't go there. I've forgiven you."

"I don't deserve it."

I raise my head and find his eyes. "Don't push me away. I need you."

"I want you in my life. I can't fathom my next step without you."

"Then stop saying we don't deserve this. Let's be together and be proud of our relationship."

He nods but lacks confidence. "I just hate that you had such low moments in your life and felt so alone. It's not right."

"I'm not alone anymore."

He kisses my forehead. "I'm here and I'll help you." Travis looks around his room, and says, "The semester is almost over, and I'll be moving out of this room. I could move in with you. Help you with rent. Have constant snuggles."

I laugh at his adorable smile.

"Move in?" It's so foreign to me. It's such a huge relationship move when all I've had is non-commitment.

"We can talk about it more," Travis adds. "Even for the summer. It'll save me from moving back to Sanford until next semester. I'm looking for work anyway, for the baby."

My gut twists. "The baby..."

He strokes my cheek and kisses me softly. "We can do this," he whispers.

I clutch his hand and nod. "We can. I was thinking about offering Naomi's room to Brittany. I want to support her, so she doesn't need to go straight into work. Give her time to think about her options, now she's leaving university."

"Has she told your parents?"

"Not yet. She's going back home to tell them in person."

"Are you scared your parents will have the same reaction towards her they did with you?"

I shrug. "I don't know. They give her so much money to live off while she is studying. They are so proud of her. Maybe with everything she's overcome, they'll let it slide?"

"That's not fair."

"That's our parents. I don't know if they'll cut her off financially or not. It'd be a lucky break if they started giving both of us money. But I'll find another job and support the two of us, regardless."

"I'll find a job," Travis replies. "I'll help you both too."

"You should concentrate on Sadie and the baby."

With that, we share a long silence. Going forward, nothing will be easy. Is that what life is? A series of hard struggles, and when you top one, another avalanches over you?

We lie down on Travis' single bed and an ounce of relief sets in as we curl up together. Being with him will make it easier. I can't imagine what life after Kellie would have been like if Travis was by my side. Maybe I wouldn't have developed a drug addiction. Would it have also meant a future at university? Would I have caved and followed my parents' wishes to study law? Or would I have found my own passion?

Maybe I needed the isolation, in those dark days, to find who I really am. And I think I'm still looking.

Three loud bangs shake Travis' dorm room door.

"Travis!" a female voice calls through the door.

Travis grunts and pulls away from me, looking at the door. He sighs and says, "That's Sadie."

I swallow uncomfortably and lift myself to sitting.

Her voice is strained and erratic. "Travis. I need to talk to you *now*."

Travis moves off the bed, and my body tightens.

My mouth dries as I ask, "You're not getting that, are you?"

"I have to see what she wants." He leans in, kisses me, and whispers, "I don't want to upset her. You know, because of the baby."

I bite inside my cheek, and my eyes sting. "I know."

He winces as he asks, "I'm sorry, can you hide in the closet?"

My eyes widen as shock puffs out of me. "What?"

"Please?" His eyes shine with guilt. "I'm so sorry. I'll get rid of her quickly. It's just the baby."

I close my eyes tight and scoot off the bed.

Travis follows me to the closet. "I'm sorry. I'm so sorry."

I swipe my eyes as I sit on the floor. Travis closes the door on me and his footsteps move to the front door. He opens it and says, "Sadie."

"What took you so long?" she snaps, moving into the room.

"Let's go for a walk," Travis suggests.

"A walk? No. I don't want to go for a walk. I need to talk to you."

"Sadie, please. Let's get some fresh air, so neither of us says anything we regret. C'mon, it'll be good for us and the baby."

Sadie huffs and stomps a foot. "Fine, c'mon, let's go."

They walk out and the door closes.

Silence. Horrible silence.

I hug my knees to my chest and hang my head. My heart pounds in the dark isolation of Travis' closet. Maybe nothing would have been different if we were still together when I finished high school.

I'm programmed to be alone.

I sit in the small space like I'm cemented to it. I'm too afraid to move. Travis is with his ex. The ex-girlfriend who is pregnant with his child. It is crazy he's staying with me instead of her.

I suck in a sharp breath and rub the pang in my heart. Shit. I'll lose him again. Another controlling girl is in the mix. Oh, Travis. Why do you involve yourself with these women? Is there something about them he likes? Does he want me to act more like them? Like, a... my stomach flips and I swallow hard... like a GiGi?

I curl into this tight ball for an eternity until the front door pushes open and Travis bursts the closet door open.

"Charli," he says breathlessly. He crouches and pulls me into his arms. "Charli, I'm sorry. I'm so, so sorry."

As my ear presses against his chest, I listen to the racing of his heart.

"I stalled her so I could come back up, but she's waiting for me."

Utter sickness swirls inside me. I'm the other woman. I'm the slut keeping this man from the woman carrying his child. I'm a disgrace.

I push him off and scramble to my feet.

"Charli, wait," he rushes, but I'm out of his dorm room in a flash.

I can't do this. I can't be this person. I can't do this to him. He deserves better than being with me.

Outside his dormitory, I keep my head down as I pace. I don't want to see her. I never want a picture of Sadie in my mind. The image of GiGi is more torment than I can bear.

As I move further into campus, my mind muddles with what to do next. I don't want to burden Brittany with all these problems. I want her to enjoy her freedom as she prepares to talk to Mum and Dad.

I pull out my phone and dial Reece. I interrupted our catch up last time, and right now, he's the only person I want to see.

"Reece," I sigh, "I don't know what to do."

We sit together in a courtyard, and he asks, "He left you to talk to his ex?"

"She's pregnant with his baby." I kick my feet below the bench and scuff my shoes against the tufts of grass. "She deserves his loyalty. He should end things with me and be with her."

"But he's not in love with her."

At that, my legs stop swinging. I plant my feet on the ground and turn to Reece, my chin dropped.

"He left her to be with you, despite the baby."

I suck in my bottom lip and shake my head. "No, he started dating me before knowing about the baby."

"So?" Reece replies. "He should be unhappy because of a baby?"

I rub the back of my neck and wince. "I'm not being fair to him."

Reece clasps onto my arm and gently shakes me. "Don't say that," he says. "You two get to make these decisions. I thought you two were happy?"

"We are. We were."

"Travis makes you happy?"

I nod as Reece lets me go. "Very happy."

"If you love him, make it work. If you don't see a future, then end it now before you get in deep."

I take in a long breath and smile at my dear friend. "You're getting so philosophical with me. Learning about life during class, are you?"

"Learning how to articulate it, I guess."

"I agree with everything you're saying," I admit. "I defended my relationship to Brittany using the same words. I even told Travis earlier that I'm proud to be with him. But being in that closet..." A sigh struggles out of me. "I just felt really selfish. I shouldn't put my happiness over others if it's going to hurt them. Sadie shouldn't feel alone or abandoned right now. That's not fair."

"Travis is with her. He hasn't abandoned her. She needed him, and he went."

"I feel guilty if she doesn't see it that way."

Reece shrugs. "You can't. You can't know. You're not inside her head."

I nudge him and try a smile. "Stop talking so much truth, would ya."

He laughs. "Sorry... not sorry."

"Thank you for hearing me out."

"Any time, you're my best friend. Are you still writing?"

"My poetry? I had started again." I swallow dryly before I add, "I thought about applying for a creative writing major."

"Here, at university?"

I nod. "Yeah. I was looking into bridging courses to finish

my HSC, but the thought of it makes me seize up."

"What do you want?" Reece asks.

The question transports me back to grade ten when I flunked a test and played hooky with Kellie. We rode our bicycles into the forest and she asked me some tough questions. I was struggling to make my parents happy, my dad in particular, and I was losing it. Kellie shook me into reality and told me to stop being fake. She was the only person who could be direct with me, and I'd respond in a positive way.

I admitted to taking amphetamines, and she chewed me out.

She asked me what I truly wanted.

I responded, "I want to be free."

And I have been. Focusing on the idea of freedom, I'm afraid I've lost connection with my relationships. Hellbent on travelling, I haven't engaged in long-term relationships with fear they'll hold me back, and I'll lose the freedom I desperately crave.

But I know Brittany needs me. And I know I want to be with Travis.

I don't want to run.

Is that all I've been doing? Running with a cover of living my own life. I was so scared in Paris. I wanted help. I wanted to know what to do. Practically and theoretically. And I want to support Travis helpfully, not just romantically. With knowledge, that will support him through nurturing a baby.

"Could you see me as a nurse?" It flies out of my mouth before my mind considers it.

Reece's head and shoulders jerk. "Huh?"

I bite into my cheek and find myself grinning. "I think I want to get into healthcare."

Reece smiles and nods. "What kind?"

I look up at the near-perfect blue sky, and shake my head, feeling the warmth radiating down as I envision Kellie nodding back at me.

"I don't know. I just know I want to help people. If I see someone in trouble, I want the ability to evaluate the situation and have confidence, knowing exactly how to help the person."

"That sounds really cool, Charli."

My body slumps with relaxation. "Thanks. I just don't know how to look into all of that."

"I can help you," Reece offers. "Maybe you can start a traineeship that will skip retaking your HSC. Or maybe some of your volunteer work will form some course credits."

"You think?"

"Worth looking into."

I lean into him and smile an immovable smile. "Thanks, Reece. You're so supportive."

His hand pats my back. "I love you, Charli. You're important to me."

As the sun forms a giant Kellie-hug around us, I shut my eyes and whisper, "I love you too."

My phone buzzes in my pocket. I pull it out and read; **New Text - Travis.**

(Travis) Hey, where are you? I need to see you.

For some reason, my stomach flips in a very uneasy way.

I show the text to Reece. "Is this a good or bad sign?"

Reece looks at my phone screen, expressionless. "It just says he needs to see you."

"Yeah, but is that a good or bad thing."

"What do you mean?"

I groan yet smile. "For a moment I forgot you were Reece."

"Huh?"

I laugh. "Don't worry. There's subtext there, but I don't think you're seeing it. Plus, I'm reading too much into it."

Reece nudges me. "It says he wants to see you. It's good."

"Could mean a breakup," I mumble.

This time he groans at me. "You just said you were gonna make it work with him. Are you bailing already?"

"Uh, no." My hands shake as I lift the phone to text. "No, I won't bail."

> **(Me)** I'm with Reece in a courtyard. I can meet you back at your room.
>
> **(Travis)** No, I need fresh air. I'll come to you. Which department are you near?

I text Travis our location and then slide the phone into my pocket. I exhale and hunch over.

Reece stands. "I'll go."

I latch onto him. "Please stay. I'm afraid I'll leave if I'm left alone to wait."

He sits and frowns at me. "Why? Why would you leave?"

I purse my lip and clench my jaw. "I'm scared."

"Of him?"

I pull back, wide-eyed. "No. Of losing him."

"Oh."

We sit together, facing forward and silent. Tension rising between us.

"Hey," Travis says with a wave as he walks towards us. He smiles at Reece. "Hey cuz."

"Hey," Reece replies, readying himself to launch off the bench.

"Everything ok?" I ask Travis. "What happened with Sadie?"

Travis rubs his shoulder as he stands in front of us. "It was a waste of time. She kept guilting me into being with her, yet she refuses to let me go to doctor's appointments with her."

I fidget on the bench seat. "So what does she want? She wants you back with her and then you can join her at the doctor's office?"

Travis shrugs and sits on the grass. "I really don't know."

"I'll leave you two to it," Reece says, standing.

"You don't have to go," Travis says to him. "Charli and I can talk about this later."

"No, I don't want to be here," Reece replies.

Travis deadpans his cousin. "Reece, I haven't seen you in ages."

"And?"

Travis swats a hand and looks away from Reece. "Fine, just go."

Reece groans and sits down next to me.

"Wow, you're staying?" I ask, surprise keeping my mouth ajar.

Reece sighs at the clouds. "Are you ok, Travis?"

Travis keeps his head down. "As much as I can be. I'm just confused."

I take a sharp breath in and stand to touch his shoulder. "Are you thinking about making it work with her?"

Travis' face shoots upward and shock coats his face as he meets my eyes. "What? No. Of course not. I want you, you silly girl."

Relief washes over me, and my grip on Travis loosens as a smile relaxes my face. "Oh. Ok. Good."

Reece smirks. "Told ya."

Travis raises an eyebrow and glances at Reece. "You were sticking up for me?"

Reece meets Travis' eyes and my heartbeat speeds up. "You two sound like you want to make it work."

Travis looks back at me, smiles, and squeezes my hand. "I really do."

I smile and nod. "Me too."

"Well, just do it," Reece says, matter-of-factly.

With that advice, uneasy laughter seeps out of Travis and me.

"It's all a little complicated," Travis hushes. "With Sadie in the way."

I chew my lip.

"But we can get through it together," Travis adds.

I smile and nod.

Travis and I sit on the bench, and he says, "I'm so sorry for doing that to you before. I shouldn't have asked you to hide. It was wrong."

I rub his thigh, eyes averted. How am I supposed to respond? Yes, it was hellish in that closet, but I didn't want to be face-to-face with Sadie.

"Now I have to go," Reece says and stands up. Neither Travis nor I move to stop him. Reece rubs my back and says, "Good luck."

I tell him thanks as he walks away.

Travis leans in close and asks, "Are we really ok?"

I kick at the patchy grass. "I want us to be ok."

"Is it bad I wish the baby didn't exist?"

A small gasp escapes me, and I meet his eyes. "No, because I wished that too."

Travis frowns and his eyes grow watery. He rests his forehead against mine and wraps his arms around me. "I think this would be way harder without you. If we never got together, I think I'd be making a huge mistake."

"Like what?"

"Making a huge commitment to Sadie right now. Making miserable future plans. It was a uni relationship, it wasn't supposed to mark the rest of my life."

I hug him tight. "It's ok to not think fondly of Sadie, but don't think of the baby as a bad thing. We will do this together. I'll help you with the baby."

"You'd do that?" his voice rises with hope.

"Of course." I smile and add, "I love you, you silly boy."

At that, Travis laughs, and he relaxes in my arms.

"You wanna get coffee or something?"

"Sure." He looks around us. "It's such a nice day. We should get takeaways, spread out on the grass, and watch the clouds move."

I kiss his cheek. "Sounds like a perfect idea."

17

Brittany

I packed about a week's worth of clothes, but I don't know how long I'll stay in Sanford. Scenario one, Mum and I get into a screaming match and I get back on a train in the city's direction. Scenario two, she helps me figure out what I really want and the direction of my next step. That could mean a week, a month, or all summer in Sanford.

I haven't missed Sanford. I haven't missed the rumours and the secrets. But I'm not in high school anymore. I just want to sit on the back deck of our beach house and gaze at the crashing ocean. Watch an orange and peach streaked sky as the sun sets. Drink fruit smoothies and let the salt air work its magic.

I'm not in high school anymore... Am I still terrified of the rumour mill? At university, I avoided parties and making new friends like I was keeping my guard up. A safety barrier against the vortex of lies and innuendo. I've been storing resistance and resentment. Maybe I can see clearly because I'm no longer with Bryce. He hated all that stuff. He never played a role in rumours about me, but being with him kept me locked in fear. That someone would talk about him, about us, or about me. And once a rumour starts, it's so hard to slow it down.

Waiting for the train doors to open, I spy Mum waiting on the Sanford Beach Station platform. With an eager smile, she waves madly. The doors open and I step onto the platform. Mum swoops her arms around me, a giddy laugh jitters her body.

"Sweetheart, I am so glad to see you," she cheers. "Why the impromptu visit? Don't you have exams to study for?"

We pull out of the hug, and I suggest, "Can we go home and talk?"

"Sure. Let me help you with your bags."

"Thanks, Mum."

The car ride home is less than fifteen minutes, but Mum fills it with two hours' worth of work stories. What is the most covert way to block my ears?

As we bring my luggage into the house via the garage, Mum says, "Of course, I spend so much more time at the office these days because this big house is so quiet."

"You wouldn't get another live-in housekeeper?"

"Not when it's only me in the house. At the moment, I have a good system. Claudette comes in twice a week to clean."

"What are you doing for food?" I smirk and add, "Or have you learnt how to cook?"

"I have a food service," Mum says with a grin. "We can use it while you're here, although I prefer to take you to restaurants when you visit."

"I don't mind," I reply. "You know, Charli has become a great cook."

"Has she?"

"You'll have to get her to cook next time she visits."

Mum sighs and looks out the kitchen window, which overlooks the back deck and the ocean that lays behind our backyard. "That is, if she'll ever come home. I don't know what else I can do to make her feel welcome here."

"What have you done to reach out to her?" I ask, sitting down in the breakfast nook and bracing myself for her attack response.

Clutching her elbows, she turns to me with exhaustion. "I've made myself too busy to visit her," Mum says. "And whenever I adjust my work schedule to free up a weekend, she's on a plane to another state or another country. I hate that I've put so much distance between myself and my daughter."

"You don't call her as often as you call me?"

Mum sits opposite me and replies, "I can ask you about school, and what subject you're studying, because I know about those things. I don't know where to begin with Charli."

"You just ask. And I'm more than what I'm studying."

She reaches across and pats my hand. "Of course. What's new with you? You wanted to talk to me about something?"

I exhale hard and quickly make eye contact. "I'm just gonna rip off the band-aid. Ok?"

She nods. "Yes."

I pull my hand away from hers and sit as tall as possible. "I hate what I'm studying."

She blinks with surprise. "A current subject, or law as a whole?"

"Law as a whole."

Mum inhales, sitting back, head turned away, and nods. When she looks back at me, she says, "Ok. Is there anything I can do to fix this? Is it a tutoring issue?"

Confidence fires through my veins as I say, "It's a happiness issue."

Mum's expression morphs into empathetic. "You're not happy, Sweetheart?"

"I haven't been for a while."

"So, what do we do?" Mum's determined eyes show her problem-solver brain grinding gears. "Do you switch majors? Do you take a gap year?"

I bite into my lip, relieved at the words I'm hearing.

"You're willing to help me figure this out?" I ask, disbelief running between each syllable.

"Of course, Brittany. You deserve to be happy."

"Do you feel the same way about Charli?"

"Of course. You equally get my love, support, and encouragement. Charli just scares me. She's impulsive, emotional, and takes action. She worries me. She takes these steps and is adventurous without making a thorough plan. I'm always scared she'll fall into traps or get taken advantage of because she doesn't think things through, and that will lead to her unhappiness."

"I never saw her like that."

"Do you believe she's happy?" Mum asks, hope radiating off her.

Mum's anxiety gives me pause. Is she? Is Charli happy?

I nod. "Happier than before she left school and moved in with Shae."

"As long as she's safe."

It's hurting my brain, so I have to ask, "Why are you so ok with me dropping out of law?"

Mum smiles and shrugs. "Maybe because I'm surprised you studied it in the first place. It wasn't a passion or a field of interest for you. It was a surprise the first time you brought it up. It was like living in a dream when you actually went through with it. I am immensely proud of you, but always wondered if it made you happy. Every time I call, you don't sound enthusiastic. Subconsciously, I must have been waiting for this conversation."

"You could have said something," I say, agitated. "I thought you'd be livid."

Mum laughs. "Of course, I want you to be a lawyer. It'd be a dream to have you by my side at the firm. But you're a creative soul. You're made for colour, not the drab beige and grey of the law."

I smirk. "Way to talk up your profession, Mum."

Mum smiles and clutches my hand. "You're a dancer, you're an artist, and you're bubbly and vibrant."

"I haven't felt bubbly and vibrant for a long time."

Her eyes dull with sadness. "Since the car accident?"

I frown and nod.

"I know, Sweetheart. I'll help however I can to get you back to feeling joyful."

"Charli has been a big help with that."

"Oh good. I want you two to be close."

I summon the courage to spit out, "We went to Paris together."

Mum's brow furrows. "Paris, France?"

I nod, bracing myself.

"What? When?"

"A few weeks ago."

"You went overseas without telling me?"

"Charli does it."

"You should say where you're going," Mum scolds. "If something happens, we will know where you are. It's a safety precaution."

"I wasn't asking for a lecture. I was telling you about how I tried to be happy."

Mum's face is flushed, I can tell she won't be helpful until the information settles in.

I get up from the table and say, "I'm going to unpack and take a shower."

"Ok, good idea."

I lug my bags upstairs, averting my eyes from the railing against the staircase, which was part of the *now dismantled* chairlift. In my bedroom, I immediately phone Charli.

"How is it?" Charli answers, her voice tense.

"Weird." It's the only way to describe it.

"How so?"

I walk across my bedroom to the balcony. I slide open the door and suck in the salty sea breeze.

"Brit?" Charli presses.

"She was fine with me dropping out of law," I say in disbelief.

"What do you mean, *fine*? Are you talking about *our* mother?"

"I know," I reply, leaning against the balcony railing. "She said she was expecting it."

"No lecture?"

"Only when I told her we went to Paris."

"You told her about that?" Charli asks sheepishly.

"She thought we were reckless because we didn't tell her we left the country."

"*Pfft*. She never cares when I travel solo."

"I think she does," I murmur.

"What did she say?"

"She just seems sad. She is working more than ever just to avoid coming home."

"She's lonely?"

I nod. "Definitely."

Charli's hard exhale rattles the phone line. "It's her own doing."

"I don't know how I'll survive being here with her," I concede. "I just want to spend my time at the beach. I'm dying for the recharge."

"Don't pressure yourself to decide on a new path. There's

no rush. I still want you to move in with me. I'll take care of the bills for as long as it takes to find your footing."

My heart warms, and my smile lifts. "Thanks, Sissy. I'm so glad to have you."

"Not a problem. Do you need to discuss how to deal with Mum?"

"No, we'll be fine. I might call back when it's time to speak with Dad."

"Are you sure you don't want me there with you?" Charli asks, worry ricocheting off her voice. "I can be there tonight or tomorrow morning."

"No. I was serious about doing this on my own. I used Bryce as a crutch until it broke us. I can't just lean on you as a replacement. I need to stand up and take care of myself."

"Ok, Brit, you got this. Good luck."

"Thanks. I'll text you later."

"Good. I'll have my phone on me."

After we say our goodbyes and end the call, I move into the bedroom and sit on the bed. Mum doesn't know about Bryce and me yet. Somehow it feels heavier to bring up. Bryce was a huge part of my high school life. He was my first boyfriend and Mum loves him. My fingers glide over the bedcovers. She even let him stay in bed with me during my recovery from surgery.

She'd better not tell me to work it out with him. How do I explain why I don't want to be with him? I glance at my wrist.

Shit.

Do I have to tell her what I did? Will she send me away like they did Charli? I'm not taking drugs, but neither was Bryce and his family sent him away. They diagnosed him with self-harm via his eating disorder. What I did was worse...

I flop back on my bed. Nup. Not telling her.

I fell asleep after wallowing became too exhausting. As I sit up on the bed, I get the woozy kinda headache after an impromptu afternoon nap. I rub my temples and look at my bedroom door. Was it a total mistake to come back here?

I wince at the thought of going downstairs. Mum was super supportive of me leaving school, or at least discontinuing law. Did I use up all her support in one hit? Will she disapprove of the changes I want to make? If I cut out school altogether, is she going to blow her top? Will she urge me to get back together with Bryce because she's lonely on her own? If I tell her about the cutting, will she force me to move in here?

With my gut screaming at me to stay on the bed, I stand. With my head pulsating with fear, I drag my feet towards the door.

Here goes nothing.

I make my way downstairs and towards the kitchen. Mum is tapping away at her laptop, the sun setting behind her.

"Did you have a good sleep?" she asks, peering over her screen.

Prompted, I rub my eyes. "Yeah. I didn't mean to fall asleep. Guess it was from travelling."

Mum sucks in a breath and moves away from the laptop. "Speaking of travelling, I'm sorry for overreacting earlier. I'm a mother, I worry. Charli is my wayward child, and I just didn't expect you to follow her adventurous spirit. I got scared and lashed out."

I smile and my body eases. "Thanks, Mum. And I guess, you didn't really lash out. I've heard you give worse lectures."

"I was thinking of ordering tacos for dinner," Mum says. "Sounds good?"

"Super good," I cheer.

Mum slips behind the laptop to place our order.

"I never would have travelled without Charli," I tell her. "But Charli didn't make me do anything. Don't take it out on her."

"I wasn't planning to, Sweetheart," Mum says with a kind smile. "I'm glad you two have a stronger bond now. And I'm glad you travelled together. It freaks me out every time Charli travels alone."

"She mostly goes with groups."

"She enters underdeveloped countries solo, and then meets up with a group of people she barely knows." Mum shakes her head. "It's frightening. She's much too brave."

"Are you jealous, Mum?" I tease.

Mum raises an eyebrow and replies, "Probably. You would never have caught me doing anything like that at eighteen."

"I want to be brave like Charli."

Mum laughs. "You two will worry me into old age."

"Whatever," I laugh.

Halfway through dinner, I drop my taco.

"Everything ok, Brit?" Mum asks.

"Bryce and I broke up," I blurt. It was eating away at me and

I didn't want the big, fat elephant at the table, depriving me of any more oxygen.

Mum drops her taco and her face pales. "When?"

"Last week," I say, sliding down my seat. "Are you disappointed?"

"No, I'm surprised. I thought everything was good between you two," she replies. "You had a fight? Oh no, he didn't cheat on you, did he?"

"Bryce? Never. He's still amazing. We just drifted apart."

"Uni life drove a wedge?"

"I guess. I just felt like I didn't have a personality anymore and became attached to him like a third arm. I need some independence."

Mum nods, searching my eyes for signs of tears and sadness. "Ok, Sweetheart. If you're sure everything's fine. But, please tell me if he hurt you. I'm here for you, Brittany."

My heart warms. "Thanks, Mum. Honestly, he did nothing wrong, we just fell out of love. The breakup was a mutual decision."

"That sounds very mature. I'm proud of you."

I wince and admit, "I wasn't very mature to begin with. I totally ghosted him when Charli and I went overseas. I didn't tell him what was going through my head."

"At least you had Charli by your side and you weren't alone."

"She actually told Bryce where we were so he wouldn't worry."

A scowl dashes across Mum's lips. "She texted Bryce, but

not your mother?"

"Don't start."

Mum sighs and picks up her taco. "It's nothing new, I guess."

"Charli told Bryce where we were so he wouldn't call and ask you," I say with mild regret. "Don't take it out on Charli. I didn't contact you either."

Mum takes a bite to avoid further discussion.

Fine by me. I pick up my taco to finish a silent dinner.

18

Charli

"It's your fault!" a girl screams in the hall as I approach Travis' dorm room. "And I want everyone to know it!"

My gut turns inside out. She's yelling at Travis.

Travis puts his hands up in defence, his face is ghostly white. "Sadie, please calm down. Come inside."

Sadie slams her hands against his chest and screams. Her fists pummel against him as she yells, "It's all your fault! Why couldn't you stay with me? You're a traitor, you bastard!"

I'm frozen as the girl's scream intensifies to an ear-piercing level. A crowd has gathered in the hall, witnessing the traumatic scene.

Travis tries to reason with her, but in a rage, she forces him away from her. People whisper back and forth, and Sadie screams again. She stomps up the hall in my direction.

I'm a stone statue as she locks eyes with me.

This is how I die.

Her eyes are red with fury and despair. She storms past me like I'm invisible.

My lungs work again. *Phew.* She doesn't know who I am.

"Charli," Travis whispers, barely audible. He beckons me over and mouths, 'come here.'

I gingerly make my way over to him as the crowd continues to whisper. What the hell did I just witness?

His expression is pure shock, and he slowly shakes his head. "The baby," he stammers.

My heart pounds with dread.

His brow furrows and his eyes dart as he makes sense of what he's about to say. "It's dead," he murmurs.

Stunned, my mouth falls open. "What?" is all I manage to say.

Still shaking his head, Travis opens his door and I follow him inside.

"That's what she was saying was your fault?" I ask, angry at how Sadie reacted in the hall.

"Yeah. Because I'm not with her."

"But you wanted to go to the appointments and help her," I reason.

"I know. She's upset. I don't blame her." Travis rubs his eyes. "It's a big deal."

"Oh, Trav," I hush and wrap my arms around him. "It's not your fault."

"I didn't want it to exist," he whispers.

"Because of me," I whisper back.

It's my fault. I kept Travis from Sadie. Without me, he'd be with her. She would have felt safe and loved... and the baby would be alive.

I killed the baby.

It's dead because of me.

I'm so selfish.

I'm an awful human being.

I don't deserve to be with him.

I don't deserve anyone.

I should have stayed alone.

Travis holds me against him, and I feel the erratic breathing jolting his chest. His arms tense, trying to remain strong when he's breaking inside.

"I brought this chaos," I whisper.

"Huh?"

I wriggle out of his arms. The agony on his face is too much to bear.

"I'm the reason you're in pain," I continue. "I shouldn't have forced my way back into your life."

He clasps my hand. "Don't talk like that. It has nothing to do with you."

"Exactly," I remark. "I inserted myself into this relationship and made everything ten times worse."

"I told you I didn't want to be with Sadie."

I stand and back away from the bed. "I've got to get out of here."

He stands. "No, don't go."

"You'll work it out. You'll work out how messed up I am and how I'll continue to hurt you."

"You did nothing wrong. I need you."

"I can't," I whisper. "I'm sorry. I need to go."

Sadness glooms over him. His head tilts as he takes me in. He breathes out with a huff.

"Ok," he whispers.

It's like being hit with a baseball bat. I leave the room and shut the door, hoping he doesn't open it. I sprint down the hall, my heart punching against my ribs.

I shouldn't have done it. That day by the film school, I shouldn't have looked for him. I shouldn't have kissed him. I shouldn't have gone to the bar. I shouldn't have seduced him and forced him into bed with me.

He deserves better than me. Sadie deserved better. I assumed she was like GiGi and deserved to be alone. But I don't know her. I wanted to hate her, but she could be lovely. She could have made Travis happy. How would I feel if someone took Travis away when I needed him the most? I'd be devastated.

I *was* devastated.

When I was dealing with my father dating someone new, I needed Travis. And then he was gone. How could I be so ruthless against another woman? I wanted him and I gave no disregard for her feelings. And that was before the baby...

Now their baby is dead.

Without me, maybe it could have survived. Had parents to look after it.

I took it all the way.

I couldn't bear to stay in his room. To see the realisation on his face. That it is all because of me. All the pain appeared when I did. I brought him nothing but harm.

Ugh. I hate this!

I make my way to the bus stop. Tears fill my eyes with the thought of going home.

What home?

I'm alone there. I can't afford it. I can't have Travis move in. The security is gone. I can't take this!

My fingers twitch with a need to take the edge off.

On the bus, I work through my need to hide. I open my phone to mywords.com and log in as *@phoenixrising* to draft a new poem.

First, I feel it in my gut,
And it manifests in my fingers,
My body screams for a smoke, or a pill,
Something to escape the world of shame.

Drinking my pain away,
Is harmful to all,
Destroyer of pride,
And never to be repeated.

I love him.
I love him too much.
Harm I will not give,
And time will reveal truth.

Break open my heart,
Search through the blood,
Find a missing part,
And discover a higher self.

If happiness is a locket,
My sister has the key,
A bond everlasting,
And stronger by the day.

With sea breeze in our hair,
And a home since birth,
A renewal is necessary,
For both to fully share.

When the bus reaches my stop, I go upstairs to my apartment to pack a bag and organise my train ticket back to Sanford.

#

Brittany meets me at the train station in Sanford. It feels crazy good for someone to meet me after travelling somewhere. I haven't had that since Nick drove me from the airport to the hospital after Brittany's accident, or when Mum drove me home from rehab.

Fun times.

Brittany hugs me hello, and says, "Mum's double-parked at the moment."

I squint at her. "Mum's here?"

"I needed her to drive," Brittany says with a shrug. "How else did ya expect me to take you home?"

"I would have just taken a taxi home," I mutter.

"Stop being so gloomy," she orders. "You are staying in the house, right? Just try to get along with her."

"I will. I was just expecting some breathing room."

On the way from the platform to the parking lot, I swear, I'm holding my breath. I spot Mum's car and my stomach cramps so hard I'm forced to release the air from my lungs.

Her figure waves through the tinted window, and I return a mediocre wave. I lift my bag into the car boot and then take the backseat.

"Hi, Charli," Mum says enthusiastically, swivelling in the driver's seat. "So glad to have you home."

"Thanks, Mum. Me too," I reply.

Brittany takes the front passenger's seat, and Mum drives out of the car park and towards home.

The ride home is mostly silent, and when we enter the house, I grab a hold of Brittany's wrist and nod towards the stairs.

"C'mon up with me?" I ask. "I need to show you something."

"Ok," she replies.

"I'll put the kettle on," Mum suggests, probably sensing the fact I'm avoiding her.

Brittany and I go upstairs and into my *now-foreign-feeling* bedroom. It's so freakin neat! The way Sophia would tidy it before I'd mess it up. The giant John Lennon poster still hangs by the desk, and an array of scattered books sit on the bookcases. I took all the photo frames with me to Sydney, so there are random vacant places.

It just doesn't feel like home anymore. And I guess that's ok.

"So, what made you decide to come home?" Brittany asks. "I was doing ok on my own."

"Oh, I know," I say, sitting on the edge of the bed. "I just needed some time to think. I didn't want to do it alone. I wanted to be with you."

"Naw, Sissy," Brittany says, giddy as she sits beside me and loops her arm with mine. "What's up?"

"Travis and the baby."

"Yeah, that won't get less messy anytime soon, will it?"

"I don't know. It's not around anymore."

"Huh? What does that mean?"

I hunch. "Sadie lost the baby."

"Oh crap," Brittany gasps. "That's horrible. How's Travis?"

"Ok, I guess. He just found out."

"So, why aren't you with him?"

"Because I didn't want to see his face when he figures out I'm the reason his life went to shit."

"What are you talking about? He's head over heels about you."

"I kept him from Sadie. She was miserable, and the baby suffered. Without me, the baby might still be alive."

"Don't talk like this. You can't know if that is true. Besides, you never said Travis couldn't see her. You were more than supportive."

"My head is just a mess right now. That's why I'm here."

Brittany rubs my arm and says, "I don't blame you. I'm sure you and Travis will get through this. Then we can go ahead as planned and all three of us live together."

The guilt swirls inside of me. Hopefulness beaming off her face. I promised to look after her. Without an income, how can I support myself, let alone her too? If Travis breaks up with me, I'll have no support. I don't know what will happen to us.

"You still want that?" I ask sheepishly.

"Of course," she cheers. "I'll try to get a job as soon as possible. I don't know how long it'll take and when I can pay my share of the rent. But that's ok, right?"

I nod, forcing a smile. "Of course."

"I'm going to have a shower," Brittany says, getting off the bed. "Go downstairs and make nice with Mum."

"Ok."

On my way into the kitchen, I can't get Brittany's excitement out of my head. I can't let her down. But is it inevitable?

Man, will disappointment ever stop being my default?

"You still like green tea?" Mum asks by the kettle.

"Ah, yeah... thanks..." I say with little interest.

"What's wrong?"

"Huh? No. Nothing."

"I see it all over your face. Are you keeping something from Brittany? You look sick or guilty."

I stare at her, everything swirling in my brain. As my thoughts continue to mash, my brain overloads and forces me to purge.

"I lost my job," I say breathlessly, my face crumpling as it readies for the onslaught of sobs.

"Oh, Charli," Mum hushes, swooping her arms around me.

"I'm sorry," I whimper, holding on to her. "I messed up."

She sways me, smoothing back my hair. "It's ok. You'll find another job. You found this one so fast. You find all your opportunities fast. When you care about something, you succeed."

I blink hard, trying to decipher what my mum is saying. I look up at her; the confusion riddled across my face.

"I don't approve of a lot of things you do," Mum says as I stare into her eyes, "but you're still standing. I've been waiting for you to tell me you made a mistake. For you to prove me right. I apologise for treating you like that."

"I don't... I don't understand."

"I didn't have any faith in you, Pumpkin," Mum says with a smile as a tear drops from her eye. "I thought leaving school would ruin your life. That you are too good to work at a bar. If you want to be a bartender, you'll easily find another job. I just want more for you, because you're incredibly smart."

"Why couldn't you have my back?" I say with a sandpaper tongue.

"I was being selfish."

I smirk as my mood lightens. "Is that where I get it from?"

Mum chuckles. "Don't forget your father. He's a good

example of that trait."

We pull out of the hug and I pat my eyes dry.

Mum swipes a thumb across my cheek and tilts her head as she says, "I want the best for you, Charlotte. You have so much potential."

I shrug and reply, "I'm thinking of going back to school."

Her expression brightens, but she reserves some enthusiasm. "Really?"

I bite into my cheek and suck in a breath. "I was thinking of becoming a nurse."

Genuine surprise and awe colours her face. "Wow. I had no idea. How did this decision come about?"

I play with my hair and eye the floor as I pick the right words. "I want to do good and contribute to the world healthily. I know what it's like to need help. When Brittany and I were alone, I saw how badly she needed help, but I didn't know how to give it to her. It was scary being so helpless. I want to learn how to be better."

Mum clasps my shoulders, her smile beams. "I'm so proud of you. You were always such an adventurous child. I always hoped you'd continue into academia, and this path will help you intellectually and practically."

"That's my hope."

"Are you wanting to go about this alone? Or do you want your father and me to help you get into school? There's bridging classes you can take to finish your high school classes."

I eye her sceptically. "You and Dad would help me?"

"We've always been willing to help you. We were just

waiting for you to open the door."

"Open the door? What are you talking about?"

"You made it very clear you wanted to move to the city on your own and get your life sorted without our help," Mum says, her jaw muscles fighting to keep her resentment in check. "When you stopped taking our calls, we reserved your money in an account. We let you explore the world on your own until you decided on a direction to take your life in."

My brain is frying. "Huh? What money?"

"Since you and Brittany were babies, we set money aside for when you finished high school. Ideally, it's for university study, but if you decided on a career without that step, we would give you the money in instalments for rent and groceries and anything else you needed."

My jaw drops. "What?"

"Your father and I have done exceptionally well financially through our careers, and it's our dream to pay it forward to you girls. We were just waiting for you to find your dream."

My mouth is still hanging open as I try to figure out how to speak words again.

Mum squeezes my hand and looks into my eyes. "I've felt alone without you in my life. I am so sorry I made you feel the same way."

I could have had the money all along? I could have funded volunteer trips with it. I wouldn't need the bar job. I wouldn't have struggled on my own.

"*Mummy,*" I whimper, throwing my arms around her neck.

My body trembles as her arms wrap around my waist.

As if reading my mind, Mum says, "I didn't want the money to go to overseas projects. I wanted it to go to you. That was me being selfish again. I wanted you to see the light, come home and go back to school. All I wanted was for you to see my path. I didn't bother to see yours."

"Mummy, I'm sorry for shutting you out," I cry.

"You've learnt a lot without me," Mum whispers. "You are resilient and self-sufficient. I didn't have the guts to go out on my own at your age. You are determined and strong, and I am so proud of you."

I pull out of the hug and find her eyes. "I'd like your help. There's a lot on my mind. Can I talk to you about them?"

Mum smiles with hope and gratitude. "Of course, Pumpkin. Anything."

We move on to the back deck and take a sunlounge each as white, fluffy clouds dawdle across the bright blue sky.

I cuddle a pillow close to my stomach as I say, "I never really told you about Travis and me breaking up."

"Oh gosh, that was quite some time ago. How old were you then? Fifteen?"

I nod. "Yeah. I never said why we broke up."

"True. I figured it was a high school romance that fizzled out. I was surprised though, you two were very smitten."

"We were... I've never forgotten the feeling, and I've always secretly wanted him back."

"Ok. Why are you bringing him up? Have you run into him lately?"

I nod again. "Yes. We started dating again."

Mum grins. "Oh, that's wonderful. I'm glad I already know him. No awkward first meetings."

"But I did something really stupid…"

Mum watches me with concern.

Something vile creeps up my throat. I groan and force myself to continue the story. "He was dating someone else when we got together."

Mum fidgets in her seat. "Oh, I see."

"He wanted to break up with her first, but I pushed for us to be together right away. I wanted to level the playing field."

"Charli, what does that mean?"

"When we were dating in high school, we went to a party and Travis got drunk. I was clear I wanted nothing more than kissing, but when he was drunk he forgot that and tried to pressure me into more."

Anger crosses Mum's face. "He forced you into sex?"

"No," I rush. "He was really, really drunk. I could stop him. But it was so disrespectful that I stopped seeing him. Even though I still loved him, I couldn't date him again because of what my friends thought."

"I don't like the sound of this one bit," Mum says, sitting tall as fury pulses through her veins. "Your father phoned me when you two were dating, voicing concerns about the age difference. I defended Travis, saying you two watched movies or studied together. We knew his parents, for crying out loud. I didn't think the concern was warranted. Uh, I'm so angry."

"Please don't be," I plead, reaching across and planting a hand on her knee. "I love him and he was remorseful right away.

He still apologises to this day."

"So this is why you feel stupid? For getting into another relationship with him?"

"Yes, but not because of what happened in high school." I drop my face to my hands. "I don't know how to say it."

"It's ok, Charli. You've come this far. There's nothing else you can say that will shock me this much."

I lift my head and wince. "Don't be so sure."

Her chin drops. "What happened?"

"His ex-girlfriend was pregnant."

"Travis is having a baby!" she exclaims.

"*Shoosh*," I hiss, my face reddening in embarrassment. "Was. Was pregnant."

Mum shakes her head. "Relay the information. Slowly. Go through the timeline."

"The lawyer in you is coming out."

"It's the only way I know to keep calm. Please, tell me everything. It's ok."

"After Travis broke up with her and we became official, his ex told him she was pregnant with his baby." Mum and I take deep breaths in. "She refused to let Travis go to doctor appointments with her until he broke up with me."

"So, you and Travis decided to stay together despite the baby?"

I nod. "Yes. We're in love."

"And you think you're ready to have a baby in your life?"

"No, but I'd figure it out. I want to help Travis. I told you before, I want to go into nursing because I truly want to help people."

"Ok, go on."

"Travis and I were committed to staying together to make it work. We talked about living together. Before I came to Sanford, he told me his ex lost the baby." Like clockwork, the tears stream from my eyes. "It's my fault, Mummy. The baby is dead because I kept Travis away from them. I shouldn't have been so selfish."

"Oh Charli," Mum whispers, moving across to my sunlounge and wrapping me in a hug. "It's not your fault, Pumpkin. Oh darling, I'm so sorry you're going through this. You shouldn't be laying so much guilt over yourself. It's not your fault."

The sobs splutter out of me as I rest my head against her shoulder.

"I thought I had him back," I cry. "But I don't deserve him."

"How can you say that? You're worthy of more love than you're getting."

"I just don't know what to do," I say, settling my nerves. "I just feel like I should set him free of me."

Mum brushes back my hair and cups my face. "You were dedicated to staying with him when the baby was alive. Why would you leave him now?"

"Because I've brought nothing but pain."

"You gave nothing but support. You didn't tell him to turn his back on her or suggest an abortion, did you?"

I gasp. "Never."

"You're not pain. You're not selfish or undeserving. If you want to be with Travis, if you really love him, I'll support you."

Mum kisses my forehead. "But, believe me, I want a quiet word with him about his intentions."

My shoulders relax, and a smile lifts my face. "I'm sure he's ready for it." I sigh and look out to the horizon. "He doesn't want to break up. He didn't want me to walk out on him. I was just scared."

"Of course. Sounds like a lot of turmoil in a short amount of time. You take your time and process everything. Thank you so much for telling me. I don't want a closed door between us anymore."

I smile and my vision blurs with happy tears. "Me either. I want to talk with you more."

"I love you, Pumpkin."

"I love you too."

"We'll have to sit down with your dad and organise access to your money, now that you're a nursing student."

"I'm not in school yet."

She kisses the top of my head. "But you will be. You achieve anything you set your mind to. That's why you didn't pursue school, despite our wishes. You had other priorities that you succeeded at."

"I would really love it if we could all be one big family. If we could be with you, Dad and Tara, and everyone is civil. I saw Nick a few weeks ago and our animosity wasn't simmering. Although, we were more concerned about Brittany than each other."

"You and Nick don't get along?"

"He and Dad get along really well. I always hated seeing

them talk things out, especially when Dad and I were arguing a lot more."

"I can relate. I don't like seeing Tara draping herself all over Rob, even though I don't want to be near him."

"Nick and I clash. Brittany thinks it's because we're too alike, but I don't see it like that."

"I don't know Nick, or Tara's other children. Perhaps that should change. Maybe our families should have more interaction."

"Imagine if we could all have Christmas together."

"Brittany would be keen for that," Mum adds.

Excitement fills my veins. "Let's talk to her about it."

19

Brittany

"Hey, I'm just checking if you're ok," Bryce says after I answer his phone call.

I smile and nod. "Yeah, I'm fine. How are you?"

"I'm fine too," he answers with a chuckle. "What have you decided with school? I heard from Nell you're dropping out?"

A sigh grumbles out of me.

"Yeah. I'm excruciatingly unfulfilled at school. Mum suggested a gap year," I explain. "I'm in Sanford at the moment."

"Oh wow. So, you are telling your parents the full story?"

"Just Mum so far. Wish me luck with Dad."

He laughs. "Good luck. You'll need it."

I grin and joke, "Thanks for the support."

"Is Charli there?"

"She got here yesterday. You two aren't still texting?"

There's a noticeable sigh before he answers. "No, I'd rather check in with you."

My smile minimises. "I don't care if you still talk to Charli. I mean, this friend thing between you and me might not last."

Ouch. I shouldn't have said it.

"Hmm," he replies. "Yeah. Maybe not. But I wanted to check in. I didn't want you feeling low and not know I'm around for you."

"Same. But I'm ok. And you're really ok?"

"Yep, I'm really ok. I'll let you get back to your family time," he says with considerable awkwardness in his tone.

"Thanks for calling. I'll see ya round."

"Bye, Brit."

I end the call and wonder if I will see him again.

"Was that Bryce?" Charli asks, standing by my bedroom door.

I chuck my phone on the bed and nod. "Yeah."

"I didn't know you two were still talking," Charli says, entering the room.

"We're trying to keep the friendship," I say with a shrug. "But I doubt he'll call again."

"You don't want to try for friends?"

"I need time away from him. Otherwise I'll continue to resent him and never feel better."

"Sounds like a healthy way to cut the cord."

"What's the latest with you and Travis? Have you called him?"

"I have," she says, sitting on my bed, devastation pulling at her face. "I didn't want to be a hypocrite after nagging you to call Bryce."

"Why did you walk out on Travis?" I ask, sitting beside her. "I thought you'd moved on from the girl who would run from tough situations."

She looks at me with fearful eyes. "This is a majorly tough situation."

"There's no baby now. It was tougher before."

"He'll resent me," Charli says, her hands balling into fists. "When he looks at me, he'll see all the damage I caused by coming back into his life."

"The boy is in love with you. He wants you."

Charli sighs and covers her face. "I just feel so selfish."

"*News flash*," I blurt. "Charli's selfish. Yeah, got that. You took up all the room in the womb and stayed a drama queen ever since."

Charli's eyebrow raises. "Drama queen? Me? Coming from you?"

"*Pah-ha!* You are *so* dramatic, Charlotte Jane. Everything is highly emotional and over-the-top. Just look at all your crazy antics throughout high school."

"Are you saying, compared, this Travis thing isn't a big deal?"

"Charli, you'd make the most microscopic incident into a mammoth deal. Just settle your emotions and look at things logically before you jump to conclusions and start running."

"You're talking to me about jumping to conclusions?"

"I'm only anxious about people talking shit because I have overheard ugly rumours about me. You can't unhear that stuff."

"Oh, believe me. Been there."

"Charli, just make up with him. Apologise for making his bad situation about yourself and be a proper girlfriend."

Charli gasp. "Oh, man. I did make it about myself. Fuck. It's his thing, and I made it about me. I am such a bitch. Why does he want to be with me?"

"Beats me," I tease.

Charli nudges me playfully. "Bitch."

My laughter rumbles out of my belly.

I jump off the bed and point at her. "Call him. Apologise."

Charli salutes me. "Yes, ma'am."

I walk to the doorway, expecting her to follow, but she hasn't budged from my bed.

"What's wrong?" I ask, leaning against the doorframe.

"I miss Sophia," she replies. "It's weird being home without her here."

"Yeah, it's totally weird. Imagine all the takeout food Mum's been eating all year."

"I promised to visit her, but I haven't," Charli says with a monster frown. "Every time I get on a plane, there's a stopover in Asia. I go to all these places, but haven't visited such a special person."

I roll my eyes and circle back to my phone. "*Ohmigawd*, like it's hard. We can call her on Skype."

Charli blinks at me. "You're an enigma, Brittany May. Sometimes you act like a timid mouse, and other times you're energetic and impulsive."

I laugh. "Ditto. You're exactly the same."

"We spent so many years trying to be different and look where it got us."

"I guess we were just born to be identical."

We wait through the seemingly never-ending rings for Sophia to answer. I have to call twice, and just when I'm about to google the time difference between Australia and the Philippines, Sophia's cheery smile brightens my phone screen.

"My cherubs!" Sophia squeals. "How are you, babies? My, my, you two look so grown up."

"Hi Sophia," Charli chimes in. "We're good. We miss you."

"How are you, Sophia?" I ask.

"I'm well, darlings. What has brought on this call?" Sophia squints at the screen. "Looks like Brittany's bedroom behind you. You two have gone back to your mother's house for a visit?"

"We needed a beach recharge," I explain.

"It's good to be home," Charli adds.

"Oh good," Sophia beams. "I'm so glad to see you two together. My goodness, Charli, more tattoos?"

"She's addicted," I snigger.

Charli nudges me. "It's creative expression."

"Don't worry, angel, you're still as beautiful as ever," Sophia says. "And you, Brittany, are looking like a natural beauty."

"Thanks, Sophia."

"How are your kids?" Charli asks. "And the rest of your family?"

"We are all doing well," Sophia answers. "Life is wonderful.

My son is going into high school next year, and my daughter is taking dance classes. We have fewer worries since your mother and father both send money every month."

"They do?" Charli and I ask in surprise.

Sophia nods. "They have been very generous. I know to them it's not much, but over here it is fantastic peace of mind."

"That's amazing," Charli says, happy tears welling in her eyes. "I'm so happy for you all."

Charli's happiness ripples over me. She's been so relaxed since Mum finally told her about the money waiting for her. I wish they had told Charli right away. I wish I had known and then could have told Charli to mend fences with our parents months ago.

"I always think of you, Brittany, when I take my daughter to ballet class," Sophia tells. "Have you taken any dance classes recently?"

"I tried," I admit. "It's so hard to find my place. I had gotten so good at dancing, it's just hard to start all over again. Like, it's embarrassing, or something."

"You'll find your feet," Sophia says optimistically. "How is school?"

I bite my lip, and then say, "I'm dropping out. It's not for me."

"Oh dear. How'd your mother take it?"

"Surprisingly well."

"What field do you think you'll move into?"

I shake my head. "I really don't know. I started sketching again, so design school is an option. I'm just sick of being in a classroom."

"Maybe you could get a traineeship, which will get you into the workforce whilst studying. Like beauty therapy. You make a superb makeup artist."

I smile. "It would be awesome to do runway makeup. Surely you wouldn't need a lot of schooling to do that?"

Sophia's cheery smile lights me up. "It's something you can look into," she says. "If you don't want to be the dancer, what about choreography? Would that excite you?"

I nod. "Yeah, perhaps. I had thought about it. It'd be cool to work with Tiffany. She sends me messages through *Instagram* every now and then. Maybe I'll catch up with her while we're staying in Sanford."

"And what about you, Charli?" Sophia asks. "Are you still at the same bar?"

"No, I got fired."

"What?" Sophia and I say at once.

Charli glances at me and murmurs, "I didn't want to worry you."

"The Travis stuff you tell me, but the job stuff you blank on?" I ask.

"Travis?" Sophia pipes up. "Travis Watkins?"

A hint of a smile appears on Charli. "We started dating again."

"Wow. This is news," Sophia says, leaning in closer to the screen.

"Yeah, we've had a few ups and downs, but I think it will work out."

I pat Charli's back, proud of her for choosing to stop running.

"Are you getting another bartender job?" Sophia asks.

Charli grins. "Can you see me as a nurse?"

Sophia giggles. "A nurse? Actually, that sounds perfect. I've watched you grow up, worrying about your sister and wanting to take care of her. You're an exceptionally caring person. I think it's a good choice for you."

"Thank you, Sophia."

"Thank you so much for calling," Sophia says, waving at the screen. "I've got to get back to the family. Take care of yourselves."

"We will. Love you," Charli and I say at once.

Sophia laughs, nodding. "Love you too. Bye for now."

The call ends and Charli and I stare at each other, grinning.

"I think I can talk to Dad now," Charli whispers.

I nod, clutching her hand. "Me too."

We go downstairs and meet Mum in the living room.

"How long will you two stay in Sanford?" Mum asks, her eyebrows twitching with the hope we'll say, *forever.*

"Maybe I can move my stuff out of the dorms and spend some time here while I figure out my next move?" I suggest, smiling. "But, ideally, I wanna live in the city. No offence, there's just more opportunities. And this town constantly reminds me of high school hell."

"You are more than welcome to stay with me. No matter the length of time," Mum says, and clasps her hands together as she sports an almighty grin. "And you, Charli?"

Charli rubs her neck in discomfort. "I dunno. I have a lot of messes to clean up. I need to figure out what is happening with my apartment, fix things with Travis, work out what I want to do with school, and get a new job."

"Pumpkin, you don't need to stress," Mum says gently. "I told you, we can provide for you. If you want, I can get you out of your lease. You can move back here while you work out how to finish high school and get into nursing school. You'd don't need to put all the pressure on yourself. That's not true freedom. You can't control everything. Please, lean on me. Let me take some of the burden, at least financially. Let me be a parent."

Charli is dumbfounded.

Overwhelmed for my sister, I hug my mother. I'm so happy they are taking care of Charli. She's been sad and alone for too long.

We all have.

"I'm selling the house," Mum blurts out.

I instantly release Mum.

"What?" Charli and I say at once.

Mum slouches, guilt twisting at her facial features. "I'm sorry. I wanted to keep it for you girls, but I can't stand being here on my own."

I take her hand. "I understand, Mum. It's a crazy big house to be alone in."

"Brit and I were talking before about how this place has lost its sense of home," Charli adds in a sympathetic tone.

Mum's posture straightens with relief. "You're both ok with this? Wherever I live, there will be space for the two of you whenever you need it."

"We want you to be happy," I say. "But, can you still live by the beach? It'll be too weird to visit and not have it as my backyard."

"I don't think there are any small homes by the water," Mum replies. "I think I'd have to move into The Heights."

"By the look on your face, it's easy to see you don't want to be that close to Dad," Charli says to Mum.

Worry slivers through my stomach. "Are we still seeing him and Tara today?"

Mum squeezes my hand. "Of course, Sweetheart. I texted him suggesting a restaurant instead of his home. I just don't think I'm ready for that."

"What restaurant?" Charli asks.

"You girls pick," Mum replies.

I look at Charli, and we grin as we answer in unison, "*Sal's.*"

Sal's Pizzeria is home to some of our best family memories. I'm warm and fuzzy just thinking about them.

When we get to *Sal's*, Dad, Tara, and our youngest step sister, Alyssa, are seated at a table. Alyssa stands from her seat and runs at us.

"Hey Lyss," Charli says, as Alyssa ambushes her with a mega hug.

"I have a drawing for you," Alyssa says, squeezing Charli's waist.

Charli's giggles as Alyssa's grip intensifies. When she finally lets go, Charli replies, "Thanks, I can't wait to see it."

Alyssa hugs me, yet much more mediocre. It's fine, I've never really gotten along with younger kids. Maybe when she's older we will get on better.

Dad and Tara move towards us. Mum steps around us and greets them first. She says hello with lame handshakes, and I can tell Tara wanted to go in for a hug.

As soon as Tara is free, I move in for that hug. Tara's hugs are the greatest.

"How are you, Brittany?" Tara asks as we embrace. "You're looking better since the last time I saw you."

"I looked bad?" I question.

"We could tell something was bothering you," Tara says, acknowledging Dad.

Dad is busy making nice with Charli. They are warm to each other, but I notice Dad scrutinising her new tattoos and Charli biting her tongue.

"Hey Dad," I interrupt, and throw an arm around him and Charli. "I'm dying for a slice."

We all sit around the table, and Tara says, "It's too bad I didn't have more notice to get Shae and Nicky back here."

"I was texting Shae yesterday on the train," Charli says. "I need to talk some things out and we are planning to meet up soon."

"And we hung out with Nick a few weeks ago," I say. I giggle before adding, "We met Ben."

Tara grins and supresses a laugh. She nods and says, "Rob and I met Ben after one of Nick's performances."

"He's quite a character," Dad remarks.

Tara brightens as she tells, "He'll be visiting Sanford with Nicky around Christmas time."

I look at Mum and then at Tara, and say, "We were talking about maybe all getting together at Christmas time."

"Both families?" Dad questions. His focus lands on Mum. "You'd be agreeable with that, Jules?"

"The girls shouldn't have to pick between us," Mum says diplomatically.

Tara raises a glass and nods at Mum across the round table. "I'd love to have our families combined, Julie."

Mum smiles and raises her glass. "To togetherness."

The rest of us are swift to raise our water glasses and meet the two mothers in the centre of the table.

Wow. I hope this works out.

Charli nudges me from the side. She smiles at me with optimism, as if telepathically replying, *'It will, if we stay in it together.'*

20

Charli

"How are you really doing, kiddo?" Dad asks as we leave *Sal's Pizzeria* and make our way to the boardwalk by the beach.

I fold my arms and send my focus through the foliage to the crashing navy blue waves beyond the sand.

"There's been a lot going on recently," I admit. "I felt certain about myself all year, but the last few weeks have left me questioning everything. I don't know if I'm just destined to make dumb mistakes repeatedly for the rest of my life."

Dad slides an arm across my shoulders as we walk along the boardwalk. "You're not dumb, Charli. You're brave."

"You don't believe that."

"You've spent a year finding yourself," he continues. "Remember when I did that? I had two fifteen-year-old daughters to take care of, but it didn't stop me. You're taking stock of your life before responsibilities set in."

"I've neglected my family and friends, and I never let any of my new relationships last." My heart aches. "Except now. You remember Travis?"

"Watkins?"

"Yeah. We started dating again, and I totally walked out on him when he needed me. I love him, Dad, but I still sabotaged our relationship."

"Do you love him enough to apologise and make it work?"

"I thought I did... But if I do, why did I leave?"

Dad kisses my forehead and smiles. "Fear."

"So, you think I can erase the mistakes and keep my relationship intact?"

"When you want something enough, you fight for it. And when you're scared, you retreat like nothing I've seen before. You went to extremes after Kellie passed away, but you've also gone to extremes to have a relationship with Brittany. Once you decide to be with Travis or not, it'll be fairly cut and dry."

"Brittany says I'm a drama queen. Maybe she's right regarding my extremeness."

"It's your adventurous spirit. Brittany doesn't have that. That's why I was happy when she studied law. I thought the structure would be good for her. She's very intelligent. She'll flourish in a creative space."

"And what do you think about me and nursing?" We'd discussed the new avenue in the restaurant, but there were so many topics to cover, we hadn't delved deep into it.

"You're active and empathetic. You have spectacular traits to be a nurse. I'm proud of you for making the choice. Perhaps you could pursue a role to help people in a similar situation you had. Dealing with drug addiction to mask emotional pain."

"Would that fall into a counselling role?"

"Not necessarily. There are lots of healthcare workers in that field. You remember them from your stay at *Lyndon House*?"

"Yeah, you're right. I was talking to Reece about it. He mentioned getting involved in overseas aid work. Like a paid position rather than a volunteer."

"That would be fantastic. It's great you have volunteered, but you know me, Charli. I believe people should be paid for their work. If you can continue on a path you love, and get paid, I'll happily support you."

"You didn't support me because I was a volunteer?"

"I was worried these organisations were taking advantage of you. I disliked you working a mediocre job and spending your earnings on projects that could be illegitimate, or taken over by a regime or government of another country."

"It wasn't like that."

"It's the sceptic in me. I wanted better for you. I'm your father, it's how I'll always feel." He clears his throat. "Speaking of better, is Travis treating you well? How long have you two been dating?"

"It's fairly new. And he's wonderful. He's attentive and caring. A real gentleman."

"The football playing, over-hormoned, party boy?"

"Because of how he acted in high school, he now holds

himself to a higher account. He's very respectful, especially towards women."

"If he's home for Christmas, bring him to the house for dinner."

I'm beaming. "I will."

When we get home, Brittany and I sit on the back deck, watching the afternoon sun change colours. Our silence is a comfort after a meal shared with both our parents and not a single argument occurred. Who would have guessed that was possible?

Heavy footsteps near from the side of the house. As I look over my shoulder, Travis appears, stepping onto the deck.

I jolt up and bound towards him. "Trav, what are you doing here?"

"She lied," he rushes, his chest heaving.

"What?" I question. "Who?"

"Sadie," he says, pulling his arms around me. "She lied to me."

My heart thuds. "She didn't lose the baby?"

He shakes his head slowly. "There was no baby. She made it all up."

"Huh?" Brittany blurts behind me.

Travis blinks at her, like she magically appeared. "Oh, hey."

"Sorry," she squeaks. "I didn't mean to interrupt."

"No, it's ok," Travis says. "You can stay." He turns his attention back to me. "There was no baby."

"That's crazy," I say, trying to fathom what this means. "How could she do that?"

Travis shrugs, bewildered. "Desperation? Scared to be alone?"

I smile as I stare into his dark chocolate eyes. "I can understand why she'd be so desperate to keep you in her life."

Dude, did Brittany just gag behind me?

"I feel like a weight has been lifted off me," Travis whispers. "Don't get me wrong, I was so mad when I overheard her friends talking about it. But now I don't have to feel guilty. It's just... done. And all I want is to be around you."

"I'm so sorry for walking out on you," I rush. "I shouldn't have left you."

Travis' lips magnetise to mine. His kiss sends warmth through my veins and untangles me from the jumbled thoughts in my head.

"Sadie fucked with us," he whispers. "Don't apologise. It wasn't either of our faults. I was just glad when you finally texted to say you were back in Sanford. Knowing the truth, I jumped in the car to get here."

"You let me leave."

His thumb sweeps under my eye. "You were devastated. I couldn't stand seeing you in pain. I told you I wouldn't let anything bad happen to you. If being with me is painful, then I'll let you leave."

I hug Travis tight. "I love you so much. I'm so relieved."

"That's hectic," Brittany murmurs.

When I leave Travis' arms, I turn around to a grinning and giddy Brittany staring at us. With every ounce of love inside me, I walk over to her and wrap her in my arms.

"Can you believe it?" I whisper.

"Can you let yourself be happy now?" she whispers back.

I pull back and look into her eyes. I cup her face and ask, "Will you be happy now?"

"With you, always."

I smile and nod. "Always."

We sit on the edge of the deck, and Travis nestles on my other side. I pivot between them and summon my courage to ask, "Are you two still keen to move into my apartment?"

"Yes," they both say at once. The massive good feeling hits me like an enthusiastic glitter cannon.

I hold on to Travis and also take Brittany's hand. "We'll be ok. We're in this together."

Travis nods at Brittany. "You'll be ok... without Bryce?"

Brittany nods, a hint of a smile appearing. "He called this morning. It was nice, although it ended awkwardly. I think it's too soon for us to maintain a friendship."

"Are you cutting him out?" I ask her.

"Not maliciously," she replies. "But for now, we just need more space. It's what we both want."

Travis kisses my cheek, and says to me, "You're not getting any space. I'm sticking to you like glue."

Brittany bursts into laughter. "*Ewwww!*"

I whack her and joke, "Such a dirty mind, Brittany May."

Brittany giggles while composing herself. "I'm so excited to move in with you. This will be a very fun new chapter."

"I am all for fun," I cheer.

Brittany clasps my hands with both of hers. My heart is

about to leap out of my chest. How did I get this lucky? I have a loving man by my side and my sister is my best friend. Her face is shiny, and wonder fills her eyes. Together, we've got this. Nothing will stop us.

To be continued...

Can't wait for the next book in the series?

Check out the prequel story, when Nick meets his boyfriend Ben, in a *Halloween* themed story you can order now!

In Chills – Releases October 2021

Want to see what happens when Brittany & Charli's blended family gets together on Christmas day? You can order the *Christmas* themed story now!

In The Spirit – Releases December 2021

Visit **www.emilybourne.net** for more information!

THANK YOU FOR READING

If you enjoyed this book, please let me know by posting a review on Amazon, Goodreads, and/or Bookbub!

To continue with the **In It Together** Series:

> #1 – In A Mirror
> #2 – In The Haze
> #3 – In It Together
> #4 – In The Beats

> *And many more to come!*

The spin-off short story collection **Holiday Together**:

> #1 – In Fiji
> #2 – In Chills
> #3 – In The Spirit
> #4 – In Secret

Other books by Emily Bourne are the **Happily After When** Series, look out for the following books:

> #1 – JAZZ
> #2 – ARIA
> #3 – CARA
> #4 – SACHI

> *And many more to come!*

NEXT BOOK IN THE SERIES

Join Nick Cooper at university, as he discovers his identity on and off the stage, and finds the true meaning of family.

THE SERIES CONTINUES

Follow along with Reece Watkins' story in book 5. Three other characters tell their stories in books 6, 7 & 8. Brittany & Charli's perspectives will return in books 9 & 10 to conclude the series.

CONNECT WITH THE AUTHOR

Visit author **Emily Bourne** in the following places:

Newsletter: www.emilybourne.net/newsletter

YouTube Search: Emily Bourne

Facebook Page: Author Emily Bourne

Instagram: @iemilybourne

Twitter: @iemilybourne